Growing in the Gray is a true "coming of age" book as the heroine, Krista or Krissy to her family, reflects back on her first year at college in Chicago. Now back at her parent's new home in her childhood state of Michigan (they have had to move to a smaller home to save money) Krissy finds herself in a small room in the basement, very different from the one she left. Planning to spend the summer relaxing and hanging out she discovers that her parents' financial situation isn't what it was, and she needs to get a summer job if she wants to go back to school.

We follow Krissy's thoughts, moods and reflections on how she has changed in the past year. We meet her friends, her boyfriend and get a taste of her life in Chicago, which is so different from what she knew back home in Michigan.

This masterly penned book is a page-turner as we are invited to hear the heroine's most intimate thoughts as she ponders her future and makes transformational choices.

I recommend this book to anyone who has had a life-changing experience growing into adulthood, and of course to those who may be taking the leap to leave home for the first time. –Joanne Tesler-Frere, Director of Program Development, Literacy Chicago

Christian Cook's novel, with endearing intimacy and deep psychological insight, elucidates a murky place on the precipice of adulthood. *Growing in the Gray* is coming of age. From a Big Boy in Michigan to an art gallery in Chicago's Wicker Park, Krista, Cook's heroine, reminds us of what it means to be eighteen, to struggle for identity, to be immersed and discovering.
—Jesse Darnay, author of *The History of Now*

Growing in the Gray pulled me in on page one. Not only did it bring me back to my youth, it also gripped my heart as I considered how Krista (the main character) processed the challenges that came her way. Christian Cook's words transformed into clear images. Her story weaved a movie in my mind as I read. It is relatable to all ages, but especially young adults trying to navigate life as they transition into adulthood. –Amy Gowans, Small Group Coach and Leader, Willow Creek Community Church, Chicago, IL

While reading *Growing in the Gray* it became increasingly difficult to stop reading. The author invites you into the life of Krista and the struggles, highs, lows, good and bad that a young woman is navigating. It felt like I was following behind Krista real time as she navigated her way through the challenges. The way the author describes the scenes, characters, and issues she's facing made this an easy read. I want an encore. –Alex McCann, Paid Social Media Manager, *Spark Foundry*

Growing in the Gray is an exceptional read. Christian Cook's human personalization of her characters are as on-point as I've ever seen, and I've read quite a few books in my time. It has the same in-depth feel as *Shopgirl* but armed with a more youthful and fresh take. *Growing in the Gray* carries on from *I Hate Gray*, and it feels as if the story has never paused. I can't wait to see how Krista thinks and operates at age 67! –Patrick Edwards, Executive Assistant, *Street Wise Magazine*

growing in the gray

Hi Khara, thank
you so much for
supporting my journey
as an author! Enjoy!

A NOVEL

CHRISTIAN COOK

IDUN

NASHVILLE, TENNESSEE

Idun is an imprint of W. Brand Publishing.

j.brand@wbrandpub.com

www.wbrandpub.com

Cover design by designchik.net

Publisher's Note: This is a work of fiction. Names, characters, places, and incidents are a product of the author's imagination. Locales and public names are sometimes used for atmospheric purposes. Any resemblance to actual people, living or dead, or to businesses, companies, events, institutions, or locales is completely coincidental.

Growing in the Gray / Christian Cook – 1st edition

Hardcover ISBN: 978-1-956906-28-8

Paperback ISBN: 978-1-956906-29-5

eBook ISBN: 978-1-956906-30-1

Kindle

LOC: 2022936283

Release date: September 6, 2022

CONTENTS

lingering

"So, how's Michigan?" Victor asked on the other end of the phone.

My head felt light from rocking back and forth on the swing set. I wondered if he could hear the screeching.

"Unfortunately, Michigan is exactly how it was when I left." I looked all around me, staring at each set of identical tan brick townhomes encircling the playground where I had decided was the best place to get some fresh air.

"Wowww, no hometown love?" he asked while chuckling.

"It's not like that, I just feel like a mold of myself here. Not the real deal, ya know?"

"I understand, I just can't relate. What are your plans for the summer?"

"Nothing in particular..." my voice trailing off as I scattered wood chips with my feet.

"I never thought there would be a day where Krista Clark didn't have a plan."

To my surprise neither did I. Between rarely being inspired here, this downgrade from our prior home to the townhouse, and already missing Chicago, I didn't know how to feel.

"That makes both of us, but what about you? Anything exciting?"

"Well, you know me, I'll be running the streets."

"Try not to catch anything while you're at it."

"Trust me, I'll do my best."

I held back a giggle. He had a way to always make me laugh, crudeness and all.

"But the summer will be over before you know it, you'll be back in the city and your boy will be here with a proper welcome back greeting," Victor assured me.

"Who's my boy?" I asked just to see his reaction.

"Ouch, you really know how to kill a man's spirit."

"A boy or a man, which one is it?" I continued to joke.

"Good question, I'll let you know when I do."

I rose from the swing as the screeching was driving me more insane than playing verbal ping pong with Victor.

Walking with a heavy heart and light feet, I heard nighttime noises that would've been drowned out by bustling trains that ran around the clock in Chicago. The chirps of crickets were now filling my ears while my eyes were being enamored by the stars that were spread throughout the blue-black sky.

"Hello...?" His voice echoed.

"Sorry about that, I just noticed there were stars in the sky, I haven't seen them in a while."

"See there's something about being there that isn't that bad."

I guess he made a point, but of course I wouldn't admit that to him in an obvious way.

"I can't even remember the last time I saw them," I said as my eyes still gazed upward.

"Actually, I can't either. Send me a pic."

"Ok."

My brows raised. I was not expecting him to care enough to ask for a picture. I bent backward a bit, making sure I got the right angle, and found just the right spot to send. Crowded with gleaming dots, not a gap of beauty in sight. God was showing out tonight.

"I just sent some," I said now with my back straight. I lowered my phone to my face, selected the speaker option, and waited for my phone to read "delivered."

"I just got them. As a photographer, I can say these are some nice shots."

"Thanksss," I responded still staring at the photos, debating if I should also post them to my story. I've been keeping a low profile since I got back and didn't feel tempted at all to broadcast grocery trips to Kroger with my mother to my virtual version of the world.

This was a complete 180 from the content I'd show-cased while I was in the city.

"Maybe I'll come and take a trip to Michigan after all."

"I highly doubt it," I stated, doing my very best to keep my skepticism to the bare minimum.

"And why is that?"

"Because you very rarely do anything that you say you're going to do with me." The words came out more direct than I desired. I did well at burying the skeptic in me, but the bitterness managed to unexpectedly creep its way through.

The silence indicated I had overstepped, but I didn't lie. My stomach began to churn, my mind was trying to come up with something light-hearted and witty to say, in hopes it would clear the air.

"So what are you going to do tomorrow?" he asked flatly.

"I have absolutely no plans, I'll probably just end up kicking it with my sisters or something."

"Well that's nice, I just have work in the morning, which means I should probably get ready to go to sleep now."

"Ok ... well, good night," I mumbled.

"Good night."

I'm almost sure that the phone hung up before he finished the word night. I didn't know who to blame though; myself for actually going down the route of honesty or him for legitimately being the reason my statement was true. I'm not sure how but now the humidity from the summer air felt thicker than before, and it was causing me to feel like the walls were closing in on me even though I was outside.

After my freshman year of college things ended with a question mark. Keeping in contact was hard, drawing the lines would have been easy if either of us had made it clear what we wanted. I convinced myself I'd wait until sophomore year to get that together once and for all. My main mission was just getting through the summer–I had faith we'd figure it out.

I trudged back to my fate. Our new family "home" that I wouldn't be able to get used to even if we lived there for 1000 years.

"Who were you talking to outside?" Valentina asked before I even fully made it through the door.

"Just a friend," I said quickly as I slid the glass door closed behind me.

"I don't have a single friend saved in my phone that makes me smile like that."

"Were you watching me the whole time? You're literally so nosy." I now felt uncomfortable, I never told anyone in my family about Victor. It would be a disaster. If I told Valentina, it would trickle down to our little sister, then our mom, and finally to the head honcho. I could imagine my dad grilling me on what

Victor's intentions were and wanting to know details about this young man that I probably didn't even know.

"Not the whole time, but long enough to know that is some special friend you have there. Plus, I'm your big sister, I'm always going to be nosy when it comes to you."

"Great," I said sarcastically.

"Your dinner is in the microwave."

I took it all in for a moment, as I stood in our mouse-trap-sized living room. The off-white furniture set that my mom hunted down and purchased from an exclusive interior designer a few towns over now looked goofy in this setting. Our oak table that occupied space adjacent to the living room looked like a misfit. No matter how much the leasing agent tried to convince us that this was a dining room, we all knew this was an extension of the living room and no well-rehearsed spiel could change that.

"Thanks for putting food up for me," I said while walking into the kitchen.

Valentina sat at one of the empty kitchen table seats. The aroma of shrimp alfredo filled my nostrils, and a smile formed on my face from ear to ear. I pressed 1 on the microwave, one minute seemed long enough since I didn't think the food had been in the microwave for very long and all these emotions fully-ignited my hunger. I couldn't wait too much longer to eat.

"Valentina ... how do you know if a boy likes you?"

"This wouldn't have anything to do with the talk you had with your friend, would it?" she asked while air quoting the word friend.

Beep. Beep. Beep. The sound of the microwave bounced off the closely constructed walls. A burst of released steam welcomed me as I opened the miniature door.

"It could be," I replied, not wanting to admit anything completely. My knowing the full answer was enough. A piece of me would be embarrassed if I confessed how much we'd played games and how much time I'd spent attempting to decipher the very mixed signals.

"Ok, since you're deliberately not giving me much to work with, I'll just say this ... if he really likes you, you won't have to second guess it. He'll make it obvious."

Sitting down at the table, my heart tensed up. Her words made me feel like I was doomed. Victor always made me second guess, and never made it obvious.

"Thanks for your insight," I managed to get out with my mouth half full of creamy alfredo sauce, noodles, and delightfully juicy shrimp.

"I can't believe you just hit me with that college term paper response, relax. What do I know anyway?"

Valentina always shocked me with her "no one really knows the answer" approach to life. I would try to mimic, but my naturally anxious nature wouldn't make it a whole twenty-four hours without failing miserably. I didn't mean to get snappy; I just couldn't help it when

7

it came to Victor. Some days I felt like I'd be better if I just got rid of these lingering feelings altogether.

"I didn't mean to sound curt; I just feel confused."

"We definitely need wine for this convo."

"Are mom and dad sleeping?" I whispered.

"We've been talking with our normal voices; I don't think whispering will solve anything now. Besides I'm grown, you're almost grown, what are they gonna do?"

She had a point, I guess.

"Did you buy any white?"

"I love how you went from being scared of getting caught, to making requests."

"I just haven't gotten into red yet, and second semester has me wanting to take a break from rosé."

"Of course, I bought white. Sauv blanc or pinot grigio?" She held up both bottles from behind the refrigerator door.

I wasn't even fully paying attention to the options she showcased; for a brief moment, my mind could only concentrate on how my family went from updated stainless-steel appliances to this sad, dingy, white refrigerator.

"Sauv blanc, please."

"Nice choice sis, this just so happens to be one of my faves."

She reached into the cupboard, grabbed two wine glasses, and I tried not to obsess over what I was actually going to do this summer. As of this moment, I was either trapped here with nothing to do or had get a job at a fast-food restaurant. Even worse than both of those options would be getting a job at the mall, where the *real* job would be ducking and dodging people I went to high school with.

I pushed my now empty plate to the right and rested my head in my folded arms which blocked the light around me. I listened to the soothing sound of wine being poured into a glass. Coming down from the high of my freshman year of college to this was not the summer I had in mind.

"This will help get you out of that head of yours for a little bit," Valentina said as she pushed the long-stemmed glass over to me by the base.

"Thanks," I mumbled as I raised my head from my arms.

"I didn't think this was possible, but I think you need this drink more than me, kid."

"What's going on with you?"

"I can't believe that's a real question," Valentina stated as she took a gulp.

I stared back at her across the table, not really sure what she would say. It seemed to me that she just floated around with little regard for those in her midst. If she had any problems you'd never know; she should work for the government because she was superb at hiding them.

"Well, I'm a 23-year-old college dropout who still lives with her parents and has no real direction." She took another gulp.

I joined her; my Victor problem now seemed completely miniscule in comparison. Aside from living with my parents, that situation was my only issue.

"You could start over anytime you wanted to, this doesn't have to be it," I preached encouragement, but I believed every word that I let roll off my tongue.

"You're right, I've been thinking about it a lot. Whatever it is, it needs to be something big. Something to completely awaken my senses."

Heavy feet began to clunk down the steps. I stiffened; Valentina remained unphased.

"Y'all can turn some of these lights off. There's no need for the living room, dining room, and kitchen lights to be on at the same time," our dad fussed as soon as he made his way completely down the stairs.

Honestly it was all like one medium-sized room, I thought it was pointless for him to list them like we lived in the Buckingham Palace.

Valentina thrusted her head back in between her shoulders and closed her eyes.

I sprung up to switch the lights off.

"I also hope the wine you both are sipping is the one that Valentina bought," he said as he surveyed the inside of the fridge, probably eyeing bottles to confirm the ones he purchased remained untouched.

"We are," I quickly retorted as I sat back down at the kitchen table.

I believe that confirmation alone sent him back up the stairs at ease with a glass of water in hand.

Valentina was still in the exact same position; I thought she would ascend to Heaven at any moment.

"Mom says he's just extra grumpy because we just moved here. I think we all need time to adjust."

"Well, while they figure out how to adjust, I'll be coming up with an escape plan. I suggest you do the same," Valentina said as she made her way upstairs.

"Good night."

"Good night, Krissy."

planning

I went from a room with crown molding along the ceilings and a walk-in closet to a space that was the equivalent to an underground storage unit. Everyday waking up here felt surreal in the worst way. It's like I went to bed aware of my reality but woke up shocked that this place was now a part of my life. No matter what my parents said or used to try to spruce this place up, it was what it was.

As I opened my eyelids and rubbed the crust that gathered from the night, I was greeted by Snoopy and Charlie Brown rocking Santa hats on the other side of the beige semi-see-through curtain that was used to give me some "privacy" from the laundry room, decor, and furniture that no longer had a place.

Buzz.

I grabbed my phone from my beloved nightstand that I had from our previous residence. It was one of the few pieces that I was able to take with me that gave me at least a sliver of feeling like home in this dust bucket of a basement.

Vic: Look at what I'm passing

It was a shot of a glass dome with greenery reaching all the way to the top. I knew the Garfield Park Conservatory when I saw it. My smile was brought on from a reminder of one of my favorite spots in the city, and also the fact that he texted me at all after our phone call that ended abruptly a few days ago. Even though he thought I was lame for going there, I thought it was strange that he'd never been especially since he's a West Side native. Some days I'd go there to work on my assignments or escape on a brutal winter day. With palm trees that seemed to go on forever and other plants that only survived in warm climates, the Conservatory always felt like spring.

Buzz.

Vic: Anytime I see it, I think of u

"Someone get me out of Michigan now," I groaned aloud as if that was the magic spell that would automatically insert me back into the city that held all of my best experiences so far.

These messages were definitely superior to a good morning text. I felt all warm and fuzzy on the inside but wasn't sure on what words to use to express that without giving away the fact that these words were the highlight of my day or summer for that matter.

My smile began to fade as the sun began to peak through the small, rectangular windows that showcased the soil that rooted the one bush that was on our side of a barely-there front yard; two steps over you were on our neighbor's front yard with the same porch steps that led to the similarly painted burgundy door and an identical bush. This repetition stretched around a circle for the entirety of the Samson Townhome complex. I thought it was vomit inducing.

I smelled green bell peppers, onions, and mushrooms coming from the vent. My mom was making her signature omelettes; that was my cue to get up, make it known I was awake before nothing was left for me.

My feet were greeted alarmingly by the cold cement floors that immediately made me yearn for the days I had heated ones that made the use of house shoes optional; here, they were mandatory.

"Good morning!" my mother exclaimed as she looked behind her and finished placing her omelette on her plate.

"Good morning, Mom," I replied while closing the door to the steps behind me and trying to look past her to ensure there was some food left.

"Morning!" I heard Valentina and Kathryn say at the same time as they sat at the kitchen table.

"Glad you could join us for breakfast this morning instead of sleeping in until God-knows-when."

"Yeah, I smelled your cooking and decided it was definitely time to get up," I said half-jokingly.

As my mom made her way to the table, I grabbed a plate from the cupboard and slipped an omelette and the last two slices of bacon on it. Bacon was a hot commodity in this household; I was grateful that there was any left at all.

"So I'm thinking about going to Michael's and getting some things to make some pieces for the house," my mom explained in between chews.

As I sat down, I admired how she was trying to make the best out of this situation, but I don't think her DIY crafts would make up for the lack of space and our neighborhood shift.

"What were you thinking?" Valentina asked as she split her omelette with a fork.

"I don't know, I could do some simple paintings or something and hang them up along the stairwell."

"That would definitely add some sparkle to the place," Valentina replied.

"Exactly how long are we supposed to be here again?" I asked flatly, simultaneously hoping it didn't crush my mother's *Design on a Dime* HGTV fantasies.

"Your father said one year, which isn't the worst but still some pieces could make this place pop."

I didn't find her statement to be untrue, but then again, my main thoughts have been focused on leaving here, the townhouse and Michigan, permanently.

"Kathryn, do you want to come with us?" my mom asked with a glistening hope in her eye, dying for one of us to meet her at her level of positivity.

"Sorry Mom, but it's a hard pass for me," Kathryn said while her neck was still tilted and scrolling on her phone; not even a smidge of eye contact was made.

"I think it could be a fun solo project for you," I interjected in an attempt to lighten the air.

"Yeah, I guess."

I would volunteer myself, but there's something about not having anything to do that makes it harder for me to commit to doing things. It's like I'm keeping my availability open for that right "thing" to come along. I did that in college, I don't know why I was doing that here. I'm pretty sure nothing better was just going to fall out of the sky.

"I might go, if you really want someone to go," Valentina said.

"No, that's ok. Krista is right, it could be nice to have a solo project."

She actually seemed convinced instead of upset; I mean, who would want to hurt their mother's feelings after she made them a delicious breakfast?

I got up from the table and made sure I washed my plate. I thought it was the least I could do.

"While you're up, can you check the mail?" my mother yelled over the running water.

"Yeah sure!"

Now in our previous neighborhood I wouldn't be caught dead checking the mail in a tattered vacation Bible school tee from middle school and purple plaid shorts from Old Navy, that almost didn't cover my butt. This place didn't matter to me, so there I was.

Even though I made the care-free decision to check the mail in my pajamas, I was pleased no one was outside. So far, I haven't had a run-in with any of our neighbors and I wouldn't mind if it stayed that way.

Women's Health Magazine, Essence Magazine, Meijer weekly sales ad, bills, bills, more bills, and my eyes widened as I saw a piece of mail from school.

"What could they want?"

I opened it, I couldn't wait for the additional two minutes it would take to get back inside. I ripped through the envelope ferociously like a child opening a present on Christmas. Surprisingly, I didn't rip the actual letter. My eyes skimmed the page up and down, but my eyes were glazing over the stark, typed words.

I took a deep breath. I started over from the top and slowed my pace down a bit.

Dear Krista,
We hope you're looking forward to the upcoming fall semester. According to your financial aid profile, you have an outstanding balance of $4,259.63.

The deadline to complete this payment is August 27th. Failure to pay will result in a financial hold on your account, and you will not be able to attend in the fall.

Read in full, hands sweating, and stomach in knots, I felt as if I was turned to stone.

"I can't believe this is happening," I sighed and re-read the typed words that left me paralyzed.

As I dragged myself toward the front porch my mind swirled, the heat intensified as I crept closer to the front door. *What was I going to do?* The thought of even mentioning this to my dad could've put me in an early grave.

"So, what will be the vibe of the art?" Valentina asked our mom as they were finishing breakfast.

All of their words sounded like background music just like my mom's day project was literally just to keep her busy; the least important thing that could be discussed right now. I plopped the stack of junk mail on the table while I gripped the letter from my school in my hand.

"Oh my gosh, what's wrong? You look like you just saw a ghost," my mom said with squinted eyes, searching my face for a clue.

Trembling, I sat back down in the same seat where I enjoyed my breakfast to deliver news I could barely say out loud.

I exhaled slowly, feeling the tension leave my bones and my heart unclench.

"Just use your words, Krista. What's going on?" Valentina urged.

"I don't know what we're going to do," I replied as I reached across the table to pass my mom the news.

My mom took the terribly torn envelope from my hands. She loathed bad news that was delayed. She much preferred you just lay it on her. I watched her as she read the letter, hoping for an expression that revealed a glimmer of hope.

"We're going to have to pray about this," my mom expressed while placing the sheet of paper down.

Definitely not the response I was expecting, but for those to be her first words further enhanced my concern. That was pretty much code for: "This is looking like it's not going to work."

"Can you at least let us know what we need to pray for, no one's actually saying anything," Kathryn droned on, she finally put her phone down.

"We owe Krista's school a good chunk of change, and without it she won't be able to go back."

"Damn! I'm sorry for the language mom, but damn," Valentina blurted.

Damn is right.

"Ok girls, grab each other's hands."

We followed her directions, clasped hands, and closed our eyes.

"Lord, we come to You in need of a miracle. Bless us with the funds needed to keep Krista in school, so she can pursue an education at the institution she has chosen. We thank You in advance for Your provision. In Jesus' name we pray, amen."

I was soothed momentarily by her words, and agreed wholeheartedly with her request, but the worry wasn't completely gone.

"So, what are we going to do?" I questioned, hoping my mother had a plan brewing.

"Well, I'm not working now so there's not much I can personally do. I'm going to have to discuss this with your dad when he's back from work."

Back in the basement, I faced the ceiling. I wondered what would become of me if I actually had to spend an extra day than I already anticipated down here; that was my version of hell on Earth. Hearing footsteps from above, conversations through the vent, and sharing a space with decorations were all too much to handle.

My stomach was doing somersaults, my leg was rocking back and forth, and my mind was running through scenarios of what would actually go down once my dad walked through the door and received the news.

I forgot to thank my mom for saying she would talk to him about it. I definitely didn't have the courage to.

I grabbed my phone and began to scroll through Victor's text thread. A piece of me wanted to tell him everything that was going on. My mind quickly pushed that thought aside as some faith chimed in and reminded me that it was too soon to tell. It wouldn't make that much sense to report something I wasn't fully sure of.

Krista: How would you feel if I didn't come back in the fall?

I stared at the question, to him it would be hypothetical but other than my concern for my future career and rotting in this basement, not seeing Victor again was my top concern. Following those concerns was the thought: *How would he feel if I didn't come back?*

Fast, light steps interrupted my thoughts.

"I had a feeling you were down here just like this. How long has it been?" Valentina asked.

"A few hours maybe."

"That is not good for you, we need to get up and get out."

"Where are we supposed to be going?"

"Let's go to Big Boy."

"So going to Big Boy is supposed to be good for me?" I asked while laughing.

"It'll be better than what you're doing now, plus we can get shakes." Valentina persuaded me with shakes and spirit fingers for special effect.

I deleted the question in the text thread between Victor and me.

"You had me at shakes."

Before heading out I looked in the mirror in our foyer. I had to make sure I looked good enough to go out with there being a chance I could run into anyone from my past. The mall, grocery store, and a place like Big Boy were all locations that had a high probability of running into ghosts from my childhood's past.

"Where are you guys going?" Kathryn asked as she was making her way downstairs.

"We're just going to get food," I replied as I examined my bun to make sure not even one coil was out of place.

"Can I come?"

"Yeah sure..." I attempted to hide my surprise that she even wanted to join us.

"Alright, you ready Miss America?" Valentina questioned while opening the front door.

"Yeah, I guess so."

"I'm coming too," Kathryn cooed as she trailed behind the both of us.

"I'm getting in the front seat," I reminded Kathryn specifically. I may not have ever gotten my license but that does not mean I would be sitting in the back.

"Fine," Kathryn grunted while texting away on her phone.

We had to walk a little extra to Valentina's car since the carport assigned to our unit was specifically designated for our parents' vehicles.

"There goes Cheryl," Valentina shouted as she pointed to her cherry red Chevy Cruze.

"I still think it's funny you named your car that."

"I think it fits, Cheryl the Chevy."

I shrugged; I couldn't really disagree.

"Krista, how come you never wanted to drive?" Kathryn questioned as we all got in the car.

I actually hated this question, partially because it was long-winded and mainly because I thought it didn't really matter.

"City girls don't need cars," Valentina mocked.

"Well, it's true," I insisted since that was one of the points that I tried convincing my parents was one of the major benefits of going off to Chicago.

"Also, the timing of actually getting the license was all off," I added.

In high school, I was balancing being on the breast cancer awareness committee, basketball team, and DECA. I didn't think I had it within me to add another obligation to the mix.

"Yeah, you can't make time for that when you're a prodigy," Valentina teased.

"Graduating high school at sixteen doesn't make me a prodigy, plus I chose to go to art school which I know everyone thinks is a joke," I reminded the both of them.

In some ways, I always felt the need to downplay or defend my accomplishments, but that intensified specifically around family or those who weren't proud of the paths they'd taken in life. Valentina just so happened to check both boxes.

What was I supposed to say? Sorry for caring about how I did in school? Sorry for being so paralyzed by overthinking that I feel the incessant need to plan everything so every small detail can go according to plan? Sorry for accomplishing to overcompensate for whatever the rest of my life was? I wasn't sorry, I just wish I didn't feel the need to be.

"Yeah but does art school cancel everything out?" Kathryn asked as she peeked her head in between the driver and passenger seat.

"Not if you actually make it," I sighed.

All the experiences I had last school year were definitely priceless, but of course when I partied instead of studying, I felt slightly guilty for not doing what I was "supposed" to do, when I wasn't pouring into my future.

"What does "making it" mean?" Kathryn air-quoted with genuine interest.

I paused. No one had actually asked me that before. I'd pictured a few different scenarios in my head before I started college and on too many occasions to recall while I was away.

"Well, if I could get a salary offer that amounts to one year of tuition after I graduate; maybe be a curator at one of my big three."

"It seems like you got it all figured out," Kathryn responded as if it was as easy as snapping my fingers.

A piece of me wanted to rest in the notion that I did have it all figured out and I would graduate and end up curating for the MCA Chicago, The Art Institute, or The Whitney. I'd dodge the post grad lull where I might end up stocking shelves somewhere until someone saw my potential and gave me a shot.

The rest of the car ride was pretty quiet. You could hear the hum of the engine and the whir of the wind as we passed trees, colonial homes that only differed in shades of brick and the colors of their shutters, and more trees. Nostalgia began to consume me as we rolled past our old subdivision. I wonder if Valentina or Kathryn noticed or did this moment just sting me? I turned my head from the window to look straight through the windshield. I wondered if things would ever go back to normal or would I have to get used to how things were until I made my own life in Chicago?

Upon entering the restaurant my nose was smacked with a heavy stench of grease and beef.

"Can we get a booth for three?" Valentina requested as we all approached the host stand.

"Sure, right this way." The hostess motioned as she grabbed three menus.

My eyes shifted from left to right trying to see if I could spot an unfriendly familiar face from K-12. To my favor, there wasn't one.

"Someone will be with you ladies shortly." She placed the laminated menus on the table while we scooched into the cushy booth.

"Ok, I hope you guys don't mind but I invited some girls from school to meet me here."

My brows squished together, and I kissed my teeth.

"Why would you do that? I thought you wanted to spend time with us," Valentina fussed. She took the words right out of my mouth.

"Well, I just thought that I should start hanging out with people before high school starts. Establish my place, so I don't look like a loser scrambling to do it at the beginning of the year," Kathryn explained.

There was clearly a lot of thought behind this and once she provided the explanation it made sense.

"Ok, I didn't think it was that serious," Valentina retorted as she scanned the menu.

"Yeah, but you haven't had your first day of high school in like ten years," Kathryn snapped back.

"I guess the times are a bit different," I intervened before this escalated into something it shouldn't have been in the first place.

"I'm just gonna get a cheeseburger and a vanilla shake," Valentina said, pushing the menu toward the middle of the table. She slumped downward and sunk into the booth.

"I'll do the same, but a strawberry shake." I also pushed my menu away.

"I'll get exactly what Krista is getting."

I looked around, walls cluttered with photographs, and everyone else seemed genuinely happy to be there. It was only we who appeared unhappy about our current lives or maybe everyone else was just good at hiding it.

I wanted to say something to lighten the mood, but I couldn't think of anything at the moment.

"Do you guys need a little more time with the menus? Are you ready to order?" Our waiter finally made his way to our table.

"We'll take three cheeseburgers, two strawberry shakes, and one vanilla shake," Valentina ordered for us all.

"Sounds good, I'll get these out the way for you and your food will be out shortly." He flashed a smile before he dashed away.

"I'm actually starving," I admitted.

"I bet, after that news earlier, you just holed up in the basement," Valentina reminded me.

"What are you gonna do?" Kathryn asked.

I didn't want to reveal how much that question turned my brain upside down.

"I don't know. Do you think dad will just pay for it?"

They both stared at me. Ok, maybe the question was stupid, but I would love to go home and have him tell me that he had enough money to cover this unexpected expense and I had absolutely nothing to worry about.

"Honestly we all know that there is a very small likelihood of that happening," Valentina spat the truth that burst the bubble of my ideal scenario.

"I guess I'm just going to have to get a job." I exhaled, that was a high probability of how this was going to go down.

"What type of job are you going to get where you can make that much money in such a short amount of time?

Again, Kathryn with a brain flipping question.

"I don't know but I better figure it out fast." I hadn't even thought about getting a job here, I was just going to chill and plan how I could stop sophomore year from being less emotionally tumultuous than freshman year.

"Ok I have three cheeseburgers, two strawberry shakes, and one vanilla," our waiter announced as he placed everything on our table.

"Thank you," Valentina replied, ripping the paper off her straw.

"You're welcome, let me know if you need anything else."

"Will do."

Biting into this burger helped me momentarily forget about everything that was going on. I wasn't thinking about money, college, my career, or the embarrassment of downgrading to the townhome.

Buzz.

Valentina, Kathryn, and I all grabbed our phones at the same time.

"Alright guys, my friends are here. Just text me when you're ready to leave," Kathryn said as she gathered her burger and drink from the table.

"Sounds good," Valentina said while chewing, and covered her mouth with a napkin.

"That kid definitely made me feel like a dinosaur," she continued once Kathryn was far enough away from the table to not hear her statement.

"I don't think she meant anything by what she said."

"I know, but it still hurt my feelings. It's like you both have some sort of mission and I don't have anything going on."

"You do realize her mission is making sure she's popular in high school," I scoffed to remind her that shouldn't be something she should be comparing herself to no matter what she's going through.

"Yeah, but at least it's important to her, and she's trying to do something about it. Then there's you with school, your goal to be a curator, and be with that boy."

"Whooooooaaa! The boy part isn't necessarily a mission," I defended, maybe a bit too passionately but Victor didn't really fit into the mission category. He was more like an undefined variable.

"Whatever you say, my point is there is something driving both of you and I have nothing."

"Well, what do you want to do?"

"That's the thing, I don't know," Valentina responded flatly and looked down at the table, shame written all over her face.

This is where I was at a loss of words. I never liked speaking on things I hadn't experienced personally, I felt like I had no right to add my input. I've pretty much always known what I wanted to do and made plans to go get whatever that was.

"Do you think you have a clue?" I inquired, hoping that it would help her think of something.

"I don't know. I keep thinking about going away. Trying something new, starting over, I see how well it went for you."

"Do you think it would be school, somewhere out of state?" I questioned as I took the last bite of my burger.

"Definitely not, I want some structure without feeling completely stifled."

That was spot on, I don't know why I mentioned school. I knew that was a sensitive topic, and I had to keep in mind that it was the route for me and not everyone.

"Well, it sounds like you have some idea of what you want. You just need to work out the kinks."

"I've been doing research on these young adult traveling groups; they seem pretty cool."

"What? So you just travel with random strangers?" I questioned, with a tone of a concerned mother.

"Oh my gosh, don't act like it's the craziest thing you've ever heard."

If it wasn't the craziest, it was definitely *one* of them. "It's just surprising, that's all."

"Well, it's just an idea, I'm just throwing it around," Valentina noted before she slurped the last drops of her vanilla shake.

"I think it's done," I chuckled.

"You're right, we should get the check," Valentina agreed.

I texted Kathryn, while Valentina tried to get the attention of our waiter.

It was time for me to face the music, get the final verdict on what was going down. If my dad wasn't home yet, he was definitely on his way. A piece of me wished I could teleport home to receive the news and the other half of me wished I could disappear from it all and pretend none of it was happening.

"Can we take the other way home?" I asked Valentina as we all got in the car. I couldn't take passing our old neighborhood again. I thought this time I might cry.

"No problem."

Entering our home after leaving the restaurant was the biggest contrast ever.

"I cannot believe this! She should've just gone to Michigan State! I heard my dad yelling from my parent's room upstairs.

My stomach sunk; this was the last thing I wanted. Hearing my parents going at each other over my life decisions always made me feel terrible about myself. This could go on all night.

"I need to find my headphones," Kathryn groaned as she stomped up the stairs.

"Don't let this get you down too much, they'll figure something out," Valentina encouraged me before she went upstairs for the night.

Naturally, of course I would let it get me down until I knew how all of this was going to turn out. In my head, there was no other option but to go back. I didn't care if I had to hit up one of those clinics to sell my blood, I'd do what was needed to get out of here.

"Craig calm down! I'm sure we have something set aside."

"I don't know how you can be so sure, Shelley, when you have no money to contribute toward setting aside!"

I stood at the bottom of the stairs hoping I would be able to hear some sort of conclusion, but after that comment I knew that wasn't going to happen anytime soon. It grew silent for a moment, so I crept up the steps; slowly and quietly, trying not to get caught so I could hear absolutely everything that would've been said when I wasn't around.

As I got to the top of the stairs I crouched down and decided it would be best to eavesdrop from the bathroom that was two doors down instead of being directly outside of their door. All I could make out were faint whimpers. My heart tightened, I hated hearing my mom cry.

"Shelley, I'm sorry. I'm just under a lot of stress. Between how business is going, living here, and now this. It's just a lot ... I'll talk to Krista in the morning."

After that, I only heard my mom sniffling.

The door opened, and I scurried from the bathroom door to the sink and at least pretended like I was brushing my teeth.

"Krista is that you?" my dad asked while leaving his bedroom.

"Yeah," I answered with a raised voice as the water was running.

"When you're done, come to the kitchen table so we can talk."

"Ok."

I decided to commit and actually brush my teeth, it provided some time to kill before I had to actually face the final decision he came up with. Each stroke against my teeth calmed my nerves, I didn't want to enter the situation all fired up. If this was my mom, letting my emotions flow could possibly get me somewhere, but it was my dad; he would hit me straight with the facts. He'd let me know exactly what it would be and what it wouldn't.

I twisted the hot water knob to the left, and the water stopped. I placed my toothbrush back in the cup with the rest of them. I was ready to hear whatever had to be said.

When I got to the bottom of the stairs, there he was drinking a glass of water with only the light above the kitchen table on.

"So, I know you want to live out whatever fantasy you've made up in your head."

I bit my cheek and refrained from interrupting. I wouldn't call going for your heart's desires a fantasy, but I didn't have a cent to my name so I sat there wondering where this could be going.

"Now you know I would've much preferred you to go to Michigan State, you had a scholarship that would've covered practically every expense."

"I understand."

"I went against my better judgement and let you go because you told me how much you wanted to go there. Now it's time for you to prove it."

"What do you mean?" I asked not knowing what he was alluding to. My fingers began to tap against my thigh, as I anticipated clarification.

"Well, if you really want something, you have to work for it. I've got my hands in a few things right now so I can't pay the amount in full. I'll provide half, I want you to get the rest."

My eyes widened; I was truly shocked to my core. I was expecting the "I told you so" portion of this conversation to go on for much longer until he began to give me a deep dive into how I could consider Chicago a part of my past.

"Ok, thank you."

"You're welcome," he stated grabbing his glass and went back upstairs.

I was still at the table, frozen by the fact that this went way better than I was expecting but I also wondered how I was going to make 2,000 and something dollars before the summer was over. Even though I was staring at a blank wall in front of me, I envisioned Lake Michigan, the Willis Tower beaming at night, and Victor. I now just realized I never texted him back.

Krista: Sorry for the late reply, I had the craziest day

He replied right away.

Vic: What happened?

Krista: It's a long story ...

Vic: With you, of course it is lol

I smiled immediately.

"Remember, no smiling until we know what this is for sure," I reminded myself outloud.

"I have no clue what I'm doing anymore," I said out loud as I walked out of my parent's house. Coming home after my first year of college I felt like I was a puzzle piece being forced into a spot it clearly wasn't made to fit in. I no longer had a bedroom but was moved down to the basement where all the other things in my parent's house that didn't have a proper place were put.

I felt the pressure to have everything mapped out, like my career plans, my own place, and a less broad plan of where I'm going with my future.

Now that Valentina was officially somewhere in Europe, things were more than dull. She couldn't be still, and she didn't want to be. I truly admired how she loved adventure and the idea of a suitcase lifestyle. My dad hated that.

"What the hell are you looking for exactly?" I heard my dad yell from the basement.

This very loud discussion took place the night before she left for her backpacking excursion.

"I don't know, but I feel like I could just find it there! I feel like it's just waiting for me!"

"How the hell would you even know what it is if you can't explain to me what it is you are looking for?"

"I feel like I would just know it when I'm there, I can't explain it, it's just something I know I will feel when it comes to me."

I could picture my dad's eyes rolling so hard they probably nearly fell onto the floor. This was a typical dad versus Valentina argument. She would try to explain how she felt in a way that she believed would persuade him that her ideas or plans he deemed to be ridiculous were great. Between the dilemma with my school and this I'm surprised he's still standing.

"That doesn't even make any damn sense!"

My dad couldn't understand why Valentina couldn't be what he thought to be normal. He would be much happier if Valentina had a steady job of some sort. Valentina would probably die if she had to go to the same place every day. She was definitely not the 9-to-5, clock-in, clock-out kind of person. Once she worked for a temp service that placed her in different offices to lend a helping hand in areas where they fell short, but even working for the temp services weren't temporary enough for her.

"I don't even know why I tried explaining this to you! I knew you wouldn't understand!"

I heard the door leading to the basement steps slam, following stomps.

"He can't stop me from going Krista, he doesn't get why no one wants to be like him," Valentina said making her way over to my bed.

"You're preaching to the choir."

"The thing is I actually told him what I was going to do, instead of asking him which was probably what threw him for a loop."

"You know he has to be the one controlling everything or everyone else around him will have a problem."

"Well, that's no longer my problem because I'll be gone in the morning."

Valentina stared at the floor for a moment, her hands trembling. She stared at the floor as if it was giving her answers, this was the first time I think I saw her look scared of anything.

"But what are you going to do there?" We had discussed the fact that she wanted to go away for a while, I just didn't think she would actually go through with it. She has always had a tendency of being flaky.

"That's the thing, I don't know which makes me believe I can't screw it up." Her eyes now off the cement floor and looking into mine, I knew she was serious.

"How long do you think you'll be gone?

"I don't know. For a while probably, I've been able to save some money just living here with them and not paying rent."

Even though I was just going to be here for the summer, I was going to miss her. I wasn't looking forward to coming back to Michigan after my freshman year of college was over, but I did like the fact that I would have time to spend with my sisters.

"Lucky you, I'll be stuck here with nothing to do and living with Dr. Evil."

We both cackled, and the sounds of laughter echoed against the poorly painted white walls, and unfinished ceiling.

"I don't think it'll be that bad. You'll have mom and Kathryn, plus you'll be back at school and running around the streets of Chicago in no time."

I shrugged my shoulders and hoped that this was going to be true. I was still nervous about getting my portion of the money I needed to return to school. I knew being here wouldn't be the same without her.

"Yeah," I said as my voice trailed off, trying to imagine what the next few months would be like here when I'd much rather be back at school or at a party, or doing anything besides being pasted to the suburbs. Things

39

weren't exactly the same way I left them after graduating high school.

"Well, don't let Dr. Evil give you too much of a hard time. You know how he gets when he gets strapped for cash."

"Hopefully things with his business get better soon." When it came down to money, I felt like I was partly to blame, I didn't pick the cheapest school to go to.

"They will, don't think about it too much, Worry Wart."

She's been calling me Worry Wart since I was a kid, unfortunately I still haven't outgrown that nickname after getting older.

"I'm not, I just can't help to think I should've just picked to go to college somewhere else, somewhere cheaper."

"No, don't let him make you think art school was a bad choice. You picked what was best for you. Once his trucking business picks back up, he'll ease up and stop being in everyone else's business."

I was praying for both. His truck business slowing down only ignited his already crabby demeanor, and less time on the road meant more time for him to monitor and judge what everyone else was doing.

I reached over my scrunched duvet to give her the tightest hug I could.

"I'm going to miss you so much."

"I'll miss you too," Valentina stated while bringing one of her arms toward her face to wipe away a tear.

Rising up from my bed with watery eyes, she sniffled but a grin began to slowly form.

"What?" I asked with furrowed brows, so confused by the swift change in emotion.

"If you didn't go to art school, how would you be the best curator in the Midwest? Don't let anyone get you down. Even though I dropped out of school, I believe in you. You'll go off to do great things."

Her words meant more to me than I could express; I hated when that happened. Sometimes even a simple thanks wasn't enough to verbalize the fact that that statement made my night and would help combat the constant fear I have that I could fail, or the constant thought of doing something else that was more "realistic" like being an accountant or driving one of my dad's trucks.

"That means a lot."

She was off the next morning. I hoped she would find whatever it was she was searching for so desperately, so she could fill this emptiness she has tried to fill by hopping from job to job, city to city, and boy to boy. I wanted her to find happiness and success for herself and prove to our dad she wasn't a screw up.

Sometimes I wanted to surprise my parents and do something they believed was strange for me to do, like get a tattoo or cut my hair, or get an edgy boyfriend to spice things up. But this wasn't my role, it was Valentina's and she played it well. Plus, if my parents had two kids like that they both would die from stress or go into cardiac arrest. Besides, being the "good" kid definitely had its advantages. Whenever I chose to be "bad" it was overlooked, and there was little to no punishment for my "crimes." I thank Valentina for that.

I decided to go for a walk and clear my head. The sun was beaming down hard, and I felt the heat on my back as I put one foot in front of the other. I've never been one to complain about how hot it is outside in the summertime, because it was summer. Where I live one doesn't know how long it'll last, and these were the days to be cherished; I'm used to wearing a North Face jacket most of the year. You tend to forget summer weather exists when it's freezing the other six months. The winters here usually started some time in November, and no one knew when they would end, we would just hope it didn't extend until June. During my senior year of high school, I remember it being cold all the way into May. People hoped for the snow and for it to be a white Christmas but every Michigander was fed up with winter by February, if not before. The same hope that was once for snow turned into prayers for at least sixty-degree weather.

I made it out of our townhouse complex and took in the familiar scenery that Southeast Michigan had to offer, which was just greenish-yellow grass, trees, and office buildings spread throughout. I couldn't help but to think if it was just a few weeks ago, I would be walking in downtown Chicago. My strolls there consisted of admiring the beautiful architecture of the skyscrapers that towered over me making me feel like I was in a movie. I made a mental note of different restaurants I wanted to try, art galleries I wanted to check out, and any other places that caught my eye before my departure. I also tried to squeeze through bustling pedestrians and not get harassed by the men on the street. That was my life from the beginning of my freshman year of college to the end of it. It all seemed like yesterday, the thoughts from this time played in my mind vividly. I caught myself, from time to time, thinking about them as I daydreamed, or if I was halfway listening to somebody from home talk about something I had zero interest in. Maybe this wouldn't be the case if I didn't feel like I was different, or if I had met people from here who had similar interests as I did while growing up, but for the most part that wasn't the case.

"Why do you even want to go here anyway?" Kathryn asked with frosty air following her words and filling the atmosphere.

We were visiting Chicago for the college's Open House, and temperatures were not exactly desirable.

At the time, I didn't notice. I felt like we were walking around a whole new world, I couldn't stop looking all around me.

"How many famous art galleries are in Michigan?"

"Uhhhh ..." her eyes were searching her brain.

"Exactly. This is my time to shine, clearly high school wasn't it, but I can just feel like this is."

We were walking a few feet behind our parents. They were holding the campus maps that were passed out at the beginning of one of the lectures; they were the only ones trying to make sure we were going in the right direction.

"Do you think dad is really going to let you go?"

"That's something I'll worry about later. For now, I'm trying to find a cute café where we can go and take pics to post. It has to be a place we don't have back at home though."

Since the school encouraged us to make the city our campus, I thought it was a great idea to concentrate on more than where classes were held and where the dorms were located, but on everything that was around me, the places I'd go take study breaks, or find cute boys. We were currently strolling down South State St. with other huddles of students and parents looking just as eager and confused as my family.

"Sounds like a good idea, we'll just have to find the perfect time to ditch mom and dad."

44

That all felt like yesterday. Now I was walking down the street, back at home smiling as these memories went through my head like a slideshow. If anyone saw me, I'm pretty sure they would think I looked like a complete idiot or that I was crazy.

I remember walking down North Michigan Avenue on my payday thinking about all the things I could do or buy. I loved passing down the streets imagining I was wealthy and prominent, because that's how I imagined the people around me. I would be passing businessmen with furrowed brows having important looking conversations on their phones. I imagined the conversation was about some million-dollar deal going wrong or something as simple as their wives were nagging them about something. Women draped in designer clothing buying even more designer garments and eating lunch with their gal pals. Then there was me, the student observing it all. I would be alone, people watching and doing some shopping. I'd go to Dylan's Candy Bar, go to Argo Tea, then I'd stop by the MCA to check out a new exhibit or admire one I've already seen. I often found by taking another look, I saw something I didn't see before and I always tried to incorporate some cultural activity I believed was nurturing to the soul. I never wanted to seem like all I wanted to do was spend money on clothing I would soon replace with something cuter or fattening myself up with candy I bought into believing was upscale.

I'd like to think when I do reach a point of financial success that those Forever21 shopping bags will turn into Salvatore Ferragamo and Yves Saint Laurent, and instead of going to the Museum of Contemporary Art to view an exhibit of a talented artist I'd be working alongside them to curate it and make their vision come alive. I'd be doing something I thought was significant with my life while helping others, looking good while doing it, and proving to myself that me pursuing a career in the arts wasn't a waste of time and my dad's money. At this time in my life nothing sounded much better than that. I would even go a step further and say that was the reason God put me on the Earth, but I still think I'm figuring out my purpose. I discussed that with Him often because I would like to know already. Making room for mistakes wasn't a luxury I had.

I went for a walk just to get out of the house. I'm pretty sure I'd been in the house for almost two weeks straight and I felt like my body was prematurely decaying. My comfy bed and covers no longer felt comfy, the covers were now starting to feel like a suffocating cocoon. On-Demand no longer felt like an amenity I missed while living in the dorms, but I felt like every episode of TV I was watching was melting my brain.

With Valentina gone, I didn't really know what to do. I didn't feel like talking to anyone. In the suburbs you only had so many options; these typically included going to the mall, the movies, a Ruby Tuesday, or your friend's house (you were a lucky one if one of your friends had a pool; that's a bonus).

In my case, friends from home that once seemed real were now only reachable through social media or text messages because we were all going on different paths in our lives and were too "busy" for one another. I also didn't keep the best contact once I started school, so trying to reunite would be a bit awkward. What was I supposed to say, "Hey, I know we haven't talked in months but do you want to come over?" Or catch them up on my family life, "Hey, so we moved from our house to a townhouse in a neighborhood not as nice as before, because my school is expensive. Want to come by?" I didn't know where to start, so I just didn't.

I was trying to understand that after college things change and I had to grasp that it was never going to be how it was in high school again. It was hard for me to stomach because that was what I was used to. But right now, I couldn't even concentrate on that. I felt like getting fresh air was no longer an option, it was a necessity. The fresh breeze welcomed my skin with a hug, and my limbs were getting the proper stretching they needed. It dawned on me that I couldn't hide in my parent's basement because my sister was gallivanting the streets of Europe, while I was probably doomed to have the lamest summer in my personal human history, and stuck where I tried to move on from.

While I was walking, I could barely believe it myself. I thought, *Wow, you're actually out of the house.* Staying indoors for two weeks straight can make you think something like that. Even though I was bummed about being home, I didn't have any assignments, I didn't have a sense of rush that Chicago filled me with, and I found it quite relaxing. It was like Chicago was the city that gave me an abundance of knots in my back, and Michigan was my masseuse that wanted to massage them all out. This was also the first time in a long time I was walking somewhere without a destination. I wasn't walking to another dorm building to visit a friend, I wasn't walking in a neighborhood that I wasn't familiar with to find an address for a party which was what a good chunk of weekends consisted of, but I was just walking to enjoy the act of going on a walk. It was refreshing. I didn't have to adjust the speed of my pace to accommodate anyone else's needs around me because I was the only person walking in Michigan. Also, walking here is not really a thing unless you're going on a nature trail. A car was the only mode of transportation, and while on my stroll I did see a few soccer moms glance at me, with a look of concern, thinking, "Where is that poor girl going?" It was annoying, but that's how things go here. Other than that, having this type of quiet without hearing heavy traffic or some older perverted man asking me, "How you doing?" was perfect. Even though it felt good, it was just different. Not having some type of time schedule was something I wasn't used to.

Time was clearly something I now had an abundance of, and a reminder that I could be doing something productive like filling my day with going to work. The only thing about that was I currently didn't have a job, and I kind of didn't want one. I debated which one would be best.

I wanted one so I wouldn't feel like I was wasting my time doing nothing in my house, and making some money of course. Let's be real, the money was the only real motive behind getting a job. A career was something different, one day I believed God would bless me with a career that I didn't dread going to but I knew that wasn't going to happen this summer, and I didn't want another placeholder job from which I couldn't gain anything. One reason for that is because I honestly hated the act of getting up and getting ready to go to work, something about it made me feel physically sick. I especially didn't want to get up early and get ready to go into a job I loathed going to. I always felt like I had to mentally prepare myself for the day, and do my best to not make up some excuse to call off. I was tired of that, and I felt heavily obligated to change it, I didn't want this to be the ongoing theme of my life. Working at Walmart or the other customer service jobs I've had, I've always had to take care of whatever a needy customer wanted help with or deal with one of my coworkers who took our minimum wage job as serious as working in the White House. I had to deal with a bitter old boss who hated me because I was a minor, and worse was dealing with another coworker who had the same position as I did and they micromanaged me like they were my boss. These were things I didn't miss, but I did miss getting a bi-weekly direct deposit into my Chase checking account; so something had to be done. I needed some motivation and a replenished work ethic, because if this laziness continued for the rest of my life I would become some bitter old boss at Walmart, or worse, just a sales associate at Walmart who had worked there for twenty years and micromanaged my coworkers because I thought I was their boss. The thought of that made me cringe, and I picked up the pace as if walking faster was going to get me any closer to some glorious future and away from the present that currently looked bleak and unpromising.

I knew I wouldn't be able to continue without a job much longer anyway. If I didn't apply the pressure, Craig definitely would. I knew how my dad was; he was not going to have me in his basement very long without making any money for myself. He was a firm believer in the "if you don't work, you don't eat" thing. Except when it came to Valentina, because I knew he didn't expect anything from her, and my younger sister Kathryn was too young to work. I was honestly surprised he hadn't been up in my face about it already, but it was only a matter of time. I would much rather have everything figured out when he speaks to me about it, than appearing like I was unprepared. If it looked like I was unprepared he would think I had zero intention of doing anything with myself and aside from me hating him judging me on my employment status, I hated coming off unprepared in general. I just turned eighteen a month ago, so I'm technically an adult now. I wanted to handle this situation as sophisticatedly as I could. After all, that *was* what I wished for when I blew out the candles on my birthday cake. I knew you don't get what you *wish* for, you get what you *work* for. Technically I didn't wish for it; I prayed for it, but even prayer without working toward what you ask is like throwing confetti into the air. Overall, I longed to be able to handle all things in a sophisticated, poised, and adultlike manner. That was my idea of cool. It was the ideal adult who was able to handle anything, and be nonchalant about everything, so the Worry Wart in me could officially die. I wonder if that will ever happen, because like all ideals it only existed in my imagination.

As I continued on my two-footed journey, I remembered blowing out my birthday candles and the smoke giving off an eerie reminder that another year of my life had passed. I didn't feel older, I didn't feel happy, but I felt anxious. It was the type of anxiousness that I felt in the pit of my stomach when I didn't know what to expect, and I didn't know what was expected of me. Smiles from my family members surrounded and encouraged me that the future was going to brighten from here.

"You should be so happy! This is just the beginning!" my mom exclaimed joyfully and hugged me.

"Krista is probably going to own her own gallery by next year and have her assistant handling her busy schedule and fetching her lattes," Valentina said jokingly.

Kathryn snapped pictures. I saw the picture later when I scrolled through my Instagram feed.

I fake smiled, it looked real to everyone else, but I felt like my face was about to crack. To me, this was the beginning of the unknown and I know Valentina was joking but I know my family expected me to be successful. But unlike Valentina, I actually planned to stick with going to school.

"Cheers to Krista and her many future successes!" my dad toasted as we all clinked our glasses.

Since I was sixteen, I had been drinking champagne on my birthday, but today my stomach was just as bubbly. Eighteen was far from old, but I felt like I should be doing more than just having dinner with my family. We weren't in a restaurant, we weren't in our 3200 sq ft. home, but the 1400 sq ft. townhouse we were all trying to get accustomed to. I pushed my cake around on my plate, which was unlike me, and my ice cream was beginning to melt into a sweet soup. I thought I'd be happy, but I wasn't where I wanted to be—a new apartment in Chicago, celebrating with my new friends, now that would be a party.

I wasn't so sure about everything that was being said. If things were looking bright, then maybe I would feel like they would, but the fact that we couldn't even get a reservation at Andiamo was the furthest thing from bright. I asked my mom, but Dr. Evil declined. While we were toasting, my dad and I made eye contact. He was actually smiling, which was nice because we didn't get much of that these days.

"Thanks for all this, guys."

"No problem, Krista," my dad said while he chewed on his pepperoni pizza. He was definitely enjoying the food he purchased.

"So, any goals for your new year?" Kathryn asked.

"Not really."

"Wow, that's surprising."

"Yeah, not like you," Valentina chimed in while sipping on her third glass of champagne.

"Well, I hope you come up with something," Craig stated while wiping sauce off of his face.

I sat still, I felt my eyes stinging as I did my best to not roll them, I didn't feel like having an argument with my family on my birthday. To refrain from saying anything back I stabbed my fork at my cake and took a bite.

"Ok guys, let's just enjoy this time we have together, it's been a while since all five of us were in one place at the same time," my mom instructed us with a smile.

I appreciate her for those words. Someone had to say it, if she hadn't, I don't know who would have.

"I'm pretty sure I'll think of something, it'll probably come to me when I'm back at school. It's kind of hard to come up with a goal when you're in a spot where you don't feel like you need any." I made sure my tone didn't rise so it wouldn't come out as disrespectful, but the words were directed to my dad while looking at Kathryn. It took a few minutes and some cake chewing to come back with the perfectly crafted statement.

By the look on my dad's face, I felt like he was ready to throw me out into the world on my own. He wanted a return on his steep investment in me and the education I was receiving, and he was paying for.

"Happy Birthday to me, right?"

Evidently, I wasn't ready for that. I was attempting to face the world full speed ahead. I hadn't wanted to have another birthday like that, I hadn't wanted to be in this townhouse, and more specifically I hadn't known what I wanted to do. I had yet to see any major differences between being seventeen and eighteen besides feeling heavily obligated to have my life together, being able to buy cigarettes and lottery tickets. Maybe I would ask Valentina to take me to pick up a few after this little shindig. Perhaps I would scratch off something that gave me some millions, I'd go away forever, and this alternate universe would no longer be a part of my life.

I hoped I hadn't peaked at seventeen. Peaked in happiness, peaked in creative flow, and peaked in the closest thing I'd ever felt to love. This birthday wasn't going to be some starting point of my life going downhill.

I hadn't been happy since I put the last box from my dorm into my dad's truck and hit I-94 East headed back to Michigan. I stared out the window practically the whole time, passing trees, rest area signs, gas stations, and my headphones in my ears with the music on full blast. My brain was preoccupied with the thoughts of the previous school year, and how I didn't really want it to end. I already missed the rush of it all and I missed Victor. The city, the art, and the only boy that I had ever let get close to me. I'd been working on reminding myself that it's just for the summer and Chicago was still going to be there when I got back, all my artist inspiration wouldn't disappear, and then there was Victor. We didn't say what we would do over the summer, but I didn't think that much would change. My feelings were unsure about that approach but how things were left, I don't think I had a choice to handle it another way. So far seventeen had my best memories, and eighteen had some big shoes to fill.

"*Huuuhhh*," I let out a breathy sigh. After thinking about that, it was all I could manage to get out. So many thoughts raced in my mind but couldn't be made into words. My mind was so busy that when I started to think about one thing, another thought interrupted without even completing the thought that came before. The sun continued to give off its rays of heat and I felt as if I was cooking in an oven; I could feel my skin getting darker. I squinted my eyes and I saw a sign for a nature trail ahead.

As I approached the trail, I noticed there was a flock of geese surrounding the entrance. I absolutely hated birds and couldn't help but to think about when I had to walk on Chicago sidewalks next to pigeons as if they were humans. From prior experience they would usually fly away when people got too close, but even the birds were different in the city. They acted like they were in charge of the sidewalk, leaving me to contort my body to avoid physical contact with them. I'm sure I looked really stupid, but I couldn't risk touching one of them. I got past the geese without any problem and did gymnastics-like stunts to avoid touching one of them. Then I saw there was a wooden bridge over a riverbank.

I took a moment to stand and take in the area around me. It was beautiful and I would've never found it if I hadn't got up and out of the house. I knew this was going to be my thinking spot.

reflecting

I continued walking across the bridge and a smirk crept across my face. I loved nature and I thought this was a hidden treasure, well maybe not *that* hidden to those who chose to leave their houses regularly, but it was to me. We had been living in the townhouse for quite some time now and I had never seen this. It felt new, like it belonged just to me.

The water was shallow and on one side, it was covered in lily pads and there were ducks swimming in lines following their mother. I wasn't expecting to see so many birds on my little adventure. Even though I wasn't particularly fond of them, out of all the birds I don't mind ducks because they never seemed to pose a real threat to me. I had never heard of someone getting attacked by ducks, I don't think that was actually a thing. Besides, they were swimming and couldn't get to me. They were in their own little world and looked very peaceful. They looked like they didn't have a care in the world. As I stared out into the distance, I couldn't help but wonder how easy the life of a duck was, they didn't worry about getting a job, college tuition, or any aspect of their future. They just swam, some on their own, some followed the leader but all of them did it with ease. It was simple, yet beautiful. In this very instant, I wouldn't mind being one, I'd spend my whole day here; not in the basement hiding away from my family's troubles or trying to figure out how I fit in a life that I left behind, or fantasizing about a life that I was trying to build but wasn't certain of how. As peaceful as this all was in the moment, I wouldn't be able to stay a duck, not knowing what I want, I would want to be a human again just a few minutes later.

I looked ahead and saw a bench a few feet away; it looked like Heaven after all that walking I had just done. My body wasn't accustomed to this level of physical activity, it felt as if a heartbeat was inside my foot; I felt the thumping in the right one and the left. That half of a mile was a bit too ambitious for me after doing absolutely nothing.

When I sat down, I stared longer at the water and saw my reflection. The blueish-green water rippled outward, distorting the view of myself. I wasn't sure how I felt when I saw it, I've always been relatively happy with the way I looked. *Have I ever wanted to lose five pounds or so?* Yeah, but I believe that's just a typical girl thing. I never really had any major complaints, but today I noticed I looked dull. This could be due to the fact of me being beyond bored with my life back at home, I had no real hobbies besides my newfound love for going to gallery openings, house party hopping, and hanging out with guys who didn't give clear signals but going along for the ride until we crashed. That was all in the other segment of my double life, here I was no one. *Which one was worse, being a girl driving too fast in a life no one guided her to steer or being bored to death and feeling invisible in a town where you lived your whole life?*

Seventeen years practically went down the drain, most were uneventful, my heart believed I traded up. My mind still weighed the pros and cons of the multitude of decisions that I couldn't seem to keep up with; they randomly popped up in my head as I made breakfast, brushed my teeth, or mindlessly watched another episode of a show that I was only halfway interested in. I was at the point where I was counting every little thing I had done to make sure I was on the right path, while not even knowing what the "right path" was.

"Did I sign up for the right classes?"

"Did I network with the right people?"

"Was this the right outfit?"

"Should I have kept in better contact with my three friends I had here?"

"Should I just run away from it all like Valentina?"

"Is Victor the one I really love?"

"Am I the one for him?"

One after the other, with no pause my thoughts raced.

My appearance was lackluster and I figured that was due to the lack of excitement in my life. I didn't look happy or have that twinkle in my eye, my mom claimed I had. I didn't look sad either, I just looked blank.

I looked to the left of me, and there was no one. I looked to my right, and no one was there.

The coast was clear.

"God, what the heck is going on with me?" I screamed in frustration. I no longer could keep this question locked away in my mind, I thought I was going crazy.

Being home brought out this feeling in me, everything essentially was the same so why did it *feel* different? Same mom, dad, siblings, just a different house, same county, same suburban vibes, same scenery. When I looked at my reflection there I was. No plastic surgery, no hair dye, no drastic appearance shift, it was just me. I knew I hadn't felt the same since I left home, but I felt better knowing I had created me and being back in Michigan with none of my vices I was a shell of me. *Was I even like this before?*

Maybe ... I could have been too detached to notice.

In all my frustration, I believed God was the only one that could answer this question, I didn't know when He was going to answer but I was sure hoping soon. I couldn't have this be one of those things that took months or years for the answer to be revealed to me in some mysterious way.

This was urgent. I needed it now or before I even asked.

"Was this a quarter-life crisis?" I'm pretty sure that's not even a thing, but if it's not I call dibs on making it up. "Wait God, I hope that's not the case. I would like to live past seventy-two."

Being this unsure all the time was not only a pain for those around me but also had been a heavy load I had to carry my whole life. Even the most minute detail, I would mull over a few times as if I was being asked, "Is that your final answer?" on *Who Wants To Be a Millionaire.*

Alone on this trail, I knew He could hear me. I just had to wait for Him to respond. That was the hard part, because it's not like I'm in the biblical days, I wasn't going to get an angel from Heaven to give me a message, a ram in a bush, or a red sea parted for me. I had to trust, follow the signs, and believe I'd be pointed in the right direction. Some days that's pretty easy for me to do, in fact it was a breeze. Then there are days where I felt like I needed to know the answer now, my stomach was churning and without knowing what to do I would be stuck in some life I never wanted, or I would be alone on a nature trail shouting at God.

I believed everyone who lived in those days had it easy. Then again, they found a way to complain too.

I didn't know what was happening with me. I felt like a diluted version of myself. I felt confused about what was going on but even more confused about why I felt so confused about what I wasn't even sure was going on with me.

I took a deep breath and exhaled; doing that always made me feel like my brain was letting off steam from all the thoughts that overwhelmed it, then I took another, and one more. Three deep breaths to center myself, to be in this moment, and not mentally in another. In those breaths, I felt the wind tickle the faint hair on my arms, I heard the quacks that were practically muted by my racing mind before, and the warm wood of the bench on my thighs.

I was here resting physically but my mind seemed like it had little to no rest at all. It had been too busy thinking of the past, which I could no longer change and the future, which I would never know for sure. Even though both of these facts bothered me I knew there was nothing I could do about it.

In Chicago, these moments were few and far between, I was always running around. Now home, when I got caught in the web of one of these mind spells my mom was always the one to keep me at ease.

"Krista what are you thinking about?" my mom asked coming down the steps with a laundry basket in her hands.

"Nothing," I lied while lying in bed on my back staring at the ceiling.

"If it's nothing then why do you look like you're constipated?"

I laughed. "Well, it *is* something, but I feel like it's something I shouldn't be concentrating on right now." Sometimes when phrases like this escaped my mind and entered into the world around me, I was afraid to be judged, even by my mom. This was mainly for the fact that I might be the only one who was thinking this and I could be the child my mom decided she needed to worry about.

My mom set the laundry basket down on the cement floor and sat down on my bed. She began to rub my head and stroke my hair back.

"I hate the fact you worry so much."

"Me too." That was the truth.

"You put yourself through unnecessary stress, you don't really have anything to be worried about."

I didn't see how she could think that. I'm in a dusty basement filled with only the stuff I had that could actually fit; everything else of mine was in a storage unit. Not only do I not want to be here, but I don't see the point.

"Mom, I feel like I have everything to worry about." That was the best that I could do, as I didn't want to offend her by talking about the place we're all living in, and not to mention the long list of other things I don't think she would understand.

"Whatever it is you're thinking about I know you'll be fine," she whispered softly and soothingly.

"How do you know?"

"I remember watching you in the living room when you were little. You would be organizing all my magazines and moving things around trying to get them just the way you thought they should be. I would just look at you and laugh and wonder what you would be when you grew up; I knew it was going to be something great."

I gazed at her while she talked. Every word that came out of her mouth was like a deposit into my self-esteem account. I loved how she smiled when talking about me like I was already someone great and worth knowing while I was in diapers.

"If you think about it, that's what you do now. Instead of organizing magazines and moving around knick-knacks you try to move things around to get your life to look the way you think it should be. You're a dream chaser and I love that about you."

"Thanks mom." After all of that I couldn't think of anything else to say. She gave me all that I needed at that moment.

"You're welcome sweetie and stop worrying so much and start praying more."

I closed my eyes and being here reminded me of sitting on the stone steps in front of Lake Michigan looking at the Chicago skyline. I would go there a lot to clear my head, think, and debate with myself over difficult situations that came up in my life. Little did I know how frequently those would come up in college, this was not mentioned in any of the orientation speeches, I would definitely have appreciated a heads up or two.

I thought it was the perfect place to go. Museum Campus felt a bit tucked away from the city, and when it was dark no one was ever there, especially in the winter; a spot I found on my own loner adventures before I discovered all the rest the city had to offer. It was also empty due to the fact no one wanted to deal with the arctic temperatures the city came with and the gusting wind directly by the lake.

The only difference between then and now was the body of water and my geographic location.

I remembered when I walked to Lake Michigan and sat on the steps for the first time while I was at war with myself. I debated if I should come back to my school after my first semester ended. I wasn't sure if going to an art school was a completely right fit for me. For starters, I didn't even know it was an art school. This was due to the fact I was focused on almost everything but the curriculum during Admitted Students Day instead of whipping my head around every thirty seconds to mentally document a landmark, another spot that caught my eye, or have Kathryn taking pictures for me to post on Instagram.

"How far do you think the Bean is from here?" Kathryn whispered while scrolling on her phone.

"I don't know, but I'm guessing not that far," I whispered back.

We finally arrived at the Auditorium Theatre.

Dimly lit, with ornate Roman paintings on the walls, white lights brightening the center stage, crowded from the main floor to the balconies.

"Let me guess, you're all here because you believe you are the creators of tomorrow?"

"Yeah!" every excited incoming freshman chanted.

"I love that enthusiasm. All that passion is going to push you through on your hard-working days here."

I wanted to let the skinny man on stage know personally that I wouldn't forget this moment. My eyes were recording everything around me, my body, a sponge, soaking in the electrifying energy that filled every inch of the place.

"Whether you're here with your parents, grandparents, cousins, or godmother, each and every person you brought here with you is a part of this journey. Our professors, counselors, and every other faculty member will be here to support you on your personal paths," his voice echoed from the mic.

"Do you think it's almost been two hours?" I heard my dad whisper as he leaned in closer to my mom.

"I'm not sure, I haven't been keeping track of the time," she managed to state through her teeth, her eyes still glued on the inspirational skinny guy giving the speech.

"I sure hope not, the last thing I want to do is pay for additional parking."

Clearly, I needed all the additional support I could get, even if it came from the school's janitor. My dad couldn't even take the time to pay attention to this moment; the moment that gave me tingles all over my body, from my toes, fingertips, and the crown of my head. I was somewhere in between giving up whatever life I had and starting the one I've been living in my head for what felt like forever, while my dad's biggest concentration was Chicago's parking prices.

"I hope every single one of you savor each moment, we can't wait to have you on campus in the fall."

I wish I could be there now.

In retrospect, I admit that I thought this was completely embarrassing, because how could someone not know what type of college they were going to? I felt like everyone got the memo and maybe I forgot to check my email or something the day the message was sent out. The fact that we didn't have a traditional campus, and the major I was interested in was Visual Merchandising should have been a clear give away. That was just the beginning of my list of problems though, I was more than halfway through the first semester and still didn't have a group of people I could call my friends. I talked to people, and I was friendly. I hung out with people from time to time, but I didn't click with people enough to consider them to be my friends. At home, I would have never guessed the start of my Chicago adventure would of been binge watching *The Vampire Diaries* on Netflix, eating "Half-Baked" Ben & Jerry's every Friday, and staring out of my window wondering if I was really cut out for this or did I make the biggest mistake of my life.

It took me some time to warm up to new people and new environments; I had to play the field a bit to see where I fit, it was quite exhausting to say the least. I also didn't fit into any of the molds of the students I had met so far.

There were people who were overly opinionated about everything, especially pertaining to the government, but didn't know anything about political protocol, and blamed everything on society. I always found this rather intriguing because people make up society, including the people who are always complaining and blaming society. I never made a comment on that verbally, I just kept it in my head. I didn't want to be the girl who made controversial comments and who had no friends. That was a bad look to me, I thought you could be one or the other but definitely not both.

There were candy-colored hair know-it-alls who dressed in soft grunge attire and overused the word *aesthetic*. Never had I ever heard that word used so much until I went to college; I almost felt like people said it just to say it.

There were people who dressed in all black and thought wearing color was stupid and drank coffee more than they breathed. Some of these people explained that wearing all black expressed their soul, so I stayed as far away from them as humanly possible. I also thought if they kept drinking coffee the way they did their teeth would be just as dark as their clothing. There were people who believed anything that was considered to be mainstream wasn't real art because the composer wasn't starving, struggling, or in some extremely dark spot in their lives; this got under my skin the most. Was everybody who made art supposed to act like they didn't care about money? Were we all supposed to act like making money wasn't important, and we would never have bills to pay, children to feed, or even feed ourselves? I have always had a vision for my life and none of them included living in a box on State Street.

There were people who wore their hair in afros and thought they were closer to their cultural roots because they chose not to straighten their hair and listened to

Erykah Badu; they would even label themselves as being Afro-centric. I don't believe in subscribing to labels. I often felt like asking all the people I met that did these things what part of Africa they were from, because I could bet my life most of them couldn't tell you. I think they just did it to fit in with each other, because they didn't fit with anybody else. I am black and I do none of these things, and I feel very culturally aware. None of these groups seemed like the place for me, and yet another divider between other black people that we clearly didn't need.

Then there were people who tried to make being depressed and emotionally detached the new "in" thing. They didn't believe in Jesus because art was the thing that they created; they believed it saved them.

I was a bit disturbed by all of them and those were just a few of them. My overall observation was everyone was trying so desperately to be different and stand out, that everyone ended up looking the same.

So, sticking to being by myself didn't seem so bad. I figured whomever I became friends with was just meant to happen, and they would come into my life when the time was right. I wasn't desperate, which I felt was a common theme that fueled a person's freshman year. Everyone wanted to find a place, have a group of friends, and not look like a loser. I definitely felt more like a loser whenever I tried to force myself with a group of people that clearly didn't fit me well. I soon learned that I would rather be alone and relatively happy, than surrounded by people and feeling miserable. Sometimes I even felt myself trying to make friends and that sometimes felt more exhausting than a full-time job, and just like every other job I had, I knew when it was time for me to quit.

This college caused me to be under the impression that the art world was just as cliquey as high school; it just had a few more pretentious assholes.

Now, things I once thought were weird were now normal in comparison to my art school experiences. Seeing someone dressed up like Lady Gaga in a meat dress, or seeing someone doing coke on the "L" train wouldn't surprise me now; it would be something I categorized as just being typical.

I recalled thinking, *if I didn't return where would I go?* I didn't like it at art school at first, but I had no other sense of direction. *If it wasn't going to be this, then what was it going to be? Where was my magic moment, where everything made sense and I felt like the place was made just for me?* I couldn't afford to keep hopping around but after a semester of failed attempts that looked like the main option. I went there because I always felt like I had big city ambitions and that was the only place where my dreams could come true.

My parents didn't want me to go to New York (which was my original plan) because it was too far, and they thought it had too many rats. I always thought it was funny they mentioned the rat population as if that stopped millions of people from living there, or the millions of kids who dreamed of inhabiting there wouldn't because of rats. I always pictured myself to be so busy there I wouldn't notice any rats. I would have stood tall, shoulders back, facing forward, strutting the streets alongside a sea of people doing the same thing. I would be going to my important job, or running errands, getting pressed juice, or doing whatever it is New Yorkers do. I had no clue; I barely knew what Chicagoans do.

As of now, Chicago got the job done while giving my parents some peace of mind because I was only about four hours away, and there was a smaller rat population than in the Big Apple.

Switching schools was also a hard decision for me because I had never envisioned going to school in Michigan. I felt like this was my time to leave here, not because I hated it and couldn't wait to leave, but because I had always lived here. I felt like this was my shot to leave and explore a place I had never been to before. I didn't want to be one of those people who just lived in one place their whole life and didn't know anything else. I mean what is the good of living the life I was given if all I did was stay in one area? Plus, I wasn't a diehard Spartan or Wolverine, so I didn't see the point in going to school in-state.

This was the only school I visited, so it made sense for me to go here. I couldn't make one of the biggest decisions of my life based off brochures, school websites, and college freshman advice videos on Youtube. I spent so much time watching those videos but just like everything else it didn't compare to the real thing, and experiencing it first-hand. The videos were made with good intentions but they were little to no help once you got to the real thing. No one can tell you what you're going to personally experience and how you're going to feel about whatever you may go through. Everyone was just trying to figure it out the best way they knew how.

On Admitted Students Day I got a good feeling from the place, I wanted that feeling back. I listened to the dazzling speeches the faculty gave. I remembered being impressed by the captivating video clips of student life, and felt invincible, as if these things motivated me to take on the world. I also remembered enjoying the cafeteria food and was surprised because I always heard that the cafeteria food in college was supposed to be disgusting. Later on I learned the school had food catered for that specific event only. It was no wonder that when I actually attended the school the food tasted like crap. I remembered getting along with the other nervous kids in my touring group, we all had this wide-eyed hopeful look on our faces. We were all looking like we expected something.

What I remembered most was the school's motto: "Live what you love." That was the thing that sold me. It was perfect to me, simple, and everything I wanted and wanted my life to be. I wanted to make sure when I went to college I was going to study something I was passionate about and would leave college with a career that aligned. I didn't want to be like the majority of people I knew who went to college and had nothing to show for it. In my eyes that would be a grave tragedy, especially since the school cost so much to attend. Going to an art school is already looked down upon by many. I would hate to be a part of the statistic who went to one and became "nothing." Needless to say, making it wasn't an option, it was mandatory.

I also got accepted into a Christian college in Indiana. I was raised Christian and grew up in the church, so I felt obligated to go. I knew I didn't want to go there though. I felt like it would be too Christian, and I wouldn't fit in. Yes, I have a relationship with God, and I pray often, but I have an edgier side that I didn't think the school would fully accept. This was me just thinking these things in my mind, and they could have been totally accepting of it, but the idea of going there wasn't appealing to me at all. I didn't want to live in a Christian bubble because the world isn't completely Christian. I needed to learn how to live cohesively with people who weren't like me for the first time in my life. I felt like college would be the perfect time to learn how to do that. Plus, I didn't want to be in the middle of Nowheresville, Indiana. I knew God wouldn't be mad at me if I didn't go.

Even though I didn't have a group of people I hung out with yet, I met a guy named Victor in the first week of November. I felt as though I couldn't leave yet. At that time, I had only known him for a couple of weeks and he was the only person that I thought I would miss if I left my school. I wanted to see where things would go.

I met Victor in the student lounge. I was reading a packet called "The Gift of Discernment." At that time, I felt like God's presence was undetectable and it was negatively affecting every aspect of my life, so I was searching for Him. I wanted to know what He had to say about me feeling out of place here, I felt like maybe the answer was in that packet. If it wasn't, maybe I would have no other choice but to go to school in Nowheresville, Indiana. Maybe I would heavily feel His presence there.

When he walked into the lounge, I remembered that I saw him in passing a few days before. That day we had made eye contact; it was that kind of awkward eye contact where both people looked at each other too long to pretend they didn't notice each other. I tried to acknowledge it by giving a toothless smirk. I felt much more comfortable doing that than waving, especially since we didn't know each other, and he smiled in return. We didn't speak to each other that day, but I could just feel that today was going to be different.

The lounge was broken up into two parts. One part was the more social area where there were plenty of tables and chairs, a pool table, a foosball table, and vending machines. The part I was in consisted of a couch, that really should be replaced because it was so tattered, and a big screen TV. He was in the other part standing in front of the vending machines, deciding what snack he wanted while I pretended not to notice him and concentrated on my reading material. I could barely concentrate on it, my eyes kept shifting from him to the words on the paper and I think I read a sentence repeatedly ten times. I was clearly no longer concentrating on the gift of discernment packet. *Sorry God.*

As I continued to try to read, I heard a voice say, "Hi."

I lowered the packet from my face, and there he was.

"Hi," I said smiling the same way I did when I saw him for the first time. I was nervous. I could tell he was coming in to talk to me and I didn't want to make a mistake and say anything stupid. I didn't let it show on the outside.

"I remember seeing you the other day. What's your name?"

"Krista, what's your's?"

"Victor. What's your major?" he asked as he sat down on the couch with his honey bun.

Since this was our first time talking, I knew the typical spiel of questions about to be asked. "What's your name and major?" were usually the first couple of ones that got the ball rolling.

"Guess," I said to spice things up, and I was naturally curious to see what he would say.

I could tell by the look on his face he was surprised I said that instead of just saying what it was.

His eyes studied me up and down as if the answer was written somewhere on my body.

"Hmmm ... is it dance?"

"Oh my gosh no," I said while laughing. I mean, I couldn't help but laugh at that because I could barely dance. I wasn't that bad, but nowhere near good enough to major in it.

"Really? You definitely look like you can dance."

I guess he said that because I was wearing shorts and my legs were looking extra-toned those days. Not having any friends or a packed social calendar gave me a lot of extra time to hit the gym in my building.

"Thanks, I'm actually a visual merchandising major, but looks can be deceiving," I said trying to be flirty, but after the words came out I wanted to punch myself in the face.

"Guess mine."

I knew this was going to be easy, every Black guy that I met here majored in something dealing with music or had the desire to be the next biggest rap star.

"Music," I said more confidently than I wanted it to come off.

He laughed because he knew why I guessed that. I'm pretty sure I wasn't the only one who believed in the "Black guy music major theory." He asked me to guess again.

I was surprised; actually, I was shocked. I let out a chuckle, because I was a little embarrassed that I couldn't think of anything else; like there was nothing else this school offered that he could possibly major in.

"I'm not going to be able to guess. What is it?"

"Photography."

I liked that a lot, I thought it was different. I liked the fact I couldn't generalize him and put him in a bubble based off the way he looked. I know I'm not supposed to do that anyway but it's something I've always done because it was easier for me, and a lot of times I've been right. I liked talking to him too. He was the first person here who made me genuinely laugh, it wasn't forced like most of the laughs produced in conversations I'd had so far in the semester. Our conversation was smooth like it was meant to happen, and I remembered thinking we would've never met if I hadn't decided to leave my dorm and switch up my scenery.

He asked me where I was from. I told him Michigan and he held up his hand pointing to his palm asking me from which part. This happened to me almost every single time I told someone where I was from. I wondered if everyone who wasn't from there thought that was fun to do. I pointed to the bottom right part of his palm. I've never had to identify where I was from on someone's hand, then again, I was always in Michigan. I asked where he was from, and he said Chicago.

"Can I have your number?"

I was typically apprehensive about giving my number out. I always feared that the person could be some psycho or a serial killer, but at this point in time I felt like I wasn't at a point where I could turn down a friend. I gave it to him then Victor and his honey bun left the lounge.

I remember the following week we hung out in his room every day. My feelings were mixed; perhaps this wouldn't happen for a girl who had experience but not only was I a virgin, I also had never hung out with a guy alone. Never did a guy come over after school, drive me home, or talk to me outside of class; this was my first time, and I was nervous. In this short amount of time, I tried to decide if he was just a friend or someone I liked, which now I know wasn't the best thing to do. I didn't know what type of person I was really dealing with; I'm sure anyone would put their best foot forward when meeting someone new. Before I could decide if I liked him, I wanted to know what he was really like. I wanted to know what type of things made him laugh, what made him happy, angry, and what he was like when he was a kid. He didn't make it easy though. He always flirted with me, and I made my best attempts to flirt back.

"You only have one letter left to guess it shouldn't be that hard," Victor said while we were playing hangman in his dorm.

I had already guessed "e" and "x," there was only one letter left. I avoided saying "s." Even though now I couldn't get the thought of us having sex out of my mind. I didn't even want to at this point, I had only known him for a week. I thought that was way too soon. Now, the thought was just lingering out there, and I only had a letter left to guess and I had to get it right or my hangman would die.

"S," I said confidently.

"Nope," Victor said as he drew the last stick leg on my guy.

"What was it then?" I questioned while looking confused.

"V. V-e-x. Vex. I can't believe you said *S*," he said with a sly smile.

I just sat there blushing.

The ducks began to quack loudly and interrupted me from cruising through my vault of memories. The sun was beginning to set, and I was getting the feeling to walk back home.

I got up from the bench and stared at the ducks before I left, and I watched them swim. They looked so free of worry; their minds weren't cluttered with memories or thoughts of things and not knowing why. I'm pretty sure they couldn't think more than one thought at a time anyway; I mean have you seen the size of a duck's head? Their brains are even smaller.

tweaking and improving

The heavy footsteps coming down the stairs interrupted my thoughts. I knew they were my dad's.

I straightened my posture and repositioned my laptop, I thought this made it look like I was doing something important.

"I hope you're doing something productive, and not on Facebook or something," he said.

I rolled my eyes. That automatically irritated me because I barely got on Facebook. The only notifications I got were from my annoying uncle who invited me to play Candy Crush; which by the way, I wished he would stop doing because he's invited me to play at least 100 times and I've never accepted so I don't know why I would any other time.

"Actually, I'm working on my resumé, I know I only have a month left of summer, which means I'll only be at home for one more month, but I can't just sit at home all day," I said to him and also to remind myself. I didn't want to sit at home all day either, being in this basement all day for the remainder of my time at home would drive me insane. Since we moved from our two-story home to our new, quaint townhouse because my parents were paying for my school expenses, I felt like I at least owed it to my dad to actively job hunt. It wasn't verbally communicated often, but there was pressure. Actually, being here and not away at school I felt it daily.

His whole demeanor changed after I told him that. It was less aggressive, and his face softened and looked more receptive to anything I could've said next. He looked proud.

"I'm happy to hear that, I want to see some of that work ethic you apply while you're at school here since I pay so much for it."

Pressure.

He was making a point. I guess I couldn't really roll my eyes and have an attitude since the reason we moved was because of my higher education cost.

"Thanks dad," I said and smiled.

"I actually came down here to check on you, I was starting to worry about you. You haven't been acting like yourself lately. You've pretty much been sleeping your life away or on your laptop." He was just stating facts, I was aware, at least I knew I had a problem.

"Yeah, I know, I'm getting back to the good old Krista. The job is just the first step."

"Good, because I can't pay for the house, the bills, your expensive school, and sluggish lifestyle all by myself on my income. I'm not Jesus. I can't feed thousands with five loaves and two fish," he said as he made his way up the stairs.

This was a typical move for my dad to make. He observed the situation for a while and then had a discussion with someone. He had been noticing my behavior the entire summer and now it had hit its peak, and he had to say something.

Today I woke up, showered, brushed my teeth, washed my face, got dressed, and woke up before noon and felt refreshingly human. This felt unusual for me because my lazy summer self was deprived of that good feeling that I once knew very well. Today was going to be different though, I had to shed my lazy summer skin before it overtook me.

I woke up with a sense of decisiveness I hadn't felt in a long time. It was something I missed dearly, and this morning it hit me like a twenty-foot wave. I could no longer be in the in-between on this matter. One reason was because I was suffering from the pains of not having any money. The other reason was if my dad asked me about my job search one more time at dinner, I think I would've choked on my food just to keep from answering any questions. I knew he'd hound me because I was technically an adult now and I hadn't been showing any signs of it. I had been staying up until 3 a.m. Waking up at 2 p.m. hoping he saved me whatever he had cooked for breakfast, lounging around on my phone for hours, showering at 7 p.m. and binge-watching Netflix until I fell asleep.

Then it would start all over, the cycle of nothingness had to stop. The other reason I knew he was on my case about it was because he had never seen me like this in my entire life. Not having some sort of plan or motivation to get off my butt wasn't like me. I remember when I turned sixteen, I was excited to celebrate my birthday, but even more excited that I was finally able to work in the state of Michigan. When we returned home from my birthday dinner at Benihana I got out of my dress, got into my comfy pajamas, and started to fill out job applications online. I wanted to work, I had a desire to grow and get things on my own; at the time, that was my start to doing that. He was proud of me then, hell I was proud of me then. I think we are both disappointed in me now.

Once again, I was in my parent's basement sitting with my feet criss-crossed on my full-size bed with my laptop open ready to get down to business.

The walls were painted white, bubbling in some spots and chipping in others. The floor was cement and always cold. The ceiling consisted of wood and housed exposed plumbing. You could hear every footstep and activity going on upstairs. It was split in half, one side was my "room," which now looked very dormlike due to the curtain dividing my side and the other side which was the laundry room and storage for all undesirable items. I took a deep breath, exhaled, and reminded myself this was only temporary.

Looking at my laptop screen I kept repeating my resumé out loud to myself. I was looking for areas I could tweek. It needed some updating.

"I am certified in Microsoft Word, Powerpoint, and Excel," I said as I typed away on my keyboard. The Excel part was a lie, but I always felt like a list was incomplete without three things, and I figured Excel couldn't be that hard to learn once I got hired.

"I work well by myself and work well in groups." I couldn't help but to laugh at this one. It wasn't a lie; I usually prefer to work alone because I find it to be easier and less hectic. But due to the excessive amount of time I'd been spending in solitude I wouldn't mind working with a team of people.

"Social media savvy." As I typed this one, I knew it was full of crap. Anyone my age knows how to tweet or post a picture to Instagram. It wasn't a science necessarily, but older people always seemed to be very impressed by it.

I always had some difficulty with making my resumé. I did enjoy talking about myself just like most people did, but it was just hard for me to do on paper without under or overestimating my skills. I wanted to seem like the perfect candidate to whomever was going to be reviewing it. All I knew right now is that I needed a job. I would like one in the field I'm studying but at this point I couldn't be too picky.

Hearing the floors creak above me motivated me more than ever to leave and never return for another summer. I don't want to sound dramatic, because it is only the summer after my freshman year of college, but I have no wish to live with my parents anymore. It was my time to go, I definitely think my parents moving me down here was them hinting that to me. Then again, that was the only space that was available for me. When we downsized to the three-bedroom townhouse, my older, nomad of a sister got a bedroom because my parents had a big hunch that she wasn't going to have a bright future and they accepted the fact she might live there forever. My parents got the master bedroom, and my younger sister got a room. It's my fault that we're here in the first place so I took the basement. If I continued to work hard at school, I was sure I would be blessed with an opportunity that would allow me to not return.

I even hoped to get an apartment off campus after the upcoming school year was over. I could't relive a summer like this ever again, almost three months had passed and I felt like I had nothing to show for it.

The idea of getting my own apartment was beautiful, but I knew my first one wasn't going to be in River North unless some miracle happend. It was one of the most expensive Chicago neighborhoods to live in, and what I considered to be a dream neighborhood. Maybe I'd be blessed enough to live there after I "made it." For now, I'd settle for a space that had enough square footage to breathe in, a neighborhood where I'd not fear being shot, and rent that wasn't so high that it made me debate having a place to live, starving to death, or paying my phone bill.

I wished I could just skip over the remainder of the summer and start the new school year already. I was ready to get back to a schedule, the city, and a place that made me feel that I was contributing toward the vision for my life, and of course, Victor. At school I felt like I was doing something important. I was working toward my future and trying to establish myself, I felt more grown up than ever there, even though being away from my parents was just the brink of what adulthood entails.

I was reminded of when my roommates Savannah and Nicolette went to go look at our first apartment. We all had no idea what we were really getting ourselves into.

"This is probably the best we're ever going to have it," I said while staring outside of our floor to ceiling windows.

The lake was in the distance, past Grant Park and peering between the Hilton Chicago and the Essex Inn, glistening in the sunlight.

"What do you mean?" Savannah asked while applying makeup in her portable light up vanity.

"I mean look around us, how are we going to afford a place like this when we move off campus?"

Our school had us absolutely spoiled with the location, views, amenities, and the fact that every class building was within walking distance. I didn't know how any of us could do anything else, I didn't want to go back to basic living. It didn't even feel like an option. Being on the seventeenth floor felt like I was far away from everything and a daily reminder that I was far from the basement.

"Truuuee," she said while stretching out each letter sound with every stroke of mascara.

"Everything is right here; I know it's expensive but I love it."

"I just need to find a place in the city, and I don't care where. All I know is I don't want to go back to Rockford."

I wasn't the only one running from something. In that sense, I felt less alone. A piece of me still felt the need to keep an image. A look as if choosing the trade of familiarity and comfort for high rise living was all worth it. Proving it to myself while simultaneously driving the point home for all my viewers back home.

"I don't want to go back to Michigan either, I just don't want to feel like I'm missing all of this right here."

"This is all a part of the dream the school tries to sell us; it doesn't feel real to me still."

This was a dream I didn't want to wake up from, I was trying to keep a positive attitude before we met up with the realtor. There were a lot of neighborhoods in Chicago, and more than downtown had to offer. Maybe I hadn't found the one that spoke to me yet.

"Well, they definitely sold it to me, what do you think we'd have to do to afford staying down here on our own?"

"I don't know... let's start selling drugs and find out," Savannah's sarcasm flowed through every word.

I stared out the window now imagining the real dream, being able to live in a place like this, without roommates.

"Anyway, didn't you pick the neighborhood we're looking at today?"

"Yeah, it's called Ravenswood."

"Ravenswood... Ravenswood..." I stated out loud while searching my brain to see if there was a memory stored there of her telling me the name of this place before or if I could recall a moment of me ever being there.

"Don't worry if you can't remember it. I picked it because I'm pretty sure we'd all like it. Plus, it's cheap," she said while applying chapstick.

The positivity I had was oozing away from my body, for some reason I didn't think I could live out my city girl fantasies in a neighborhood I couldn't even remember being mentioned.

"Isn't it time to meet Nicolette in the lobby?"

Let's just get this over with.

"Do you have your key card?" she asked as she stood up from her desk.

I patted my pants pockets, and it wasn't there. Patting my jacket pocket, I felt my pouch with my ID, keycard, debit card and lip balm.

"Check," I locked myself out for what felt like every other day the first two weeks of school.

"Good, I couldn't let you leave without making sure."

"Thanks for the reminder."

Leaving out of here everyday, I had a mental checklist, this just was just another thing I could add on the list of things I felt the need to do here that I didn't at home.

Keys?

Check.

Assignments done?

Check.

Ventra Card?

Check.

There was always something I needed, more responsibility I was accustomed to taking on. Some days it felt like second nature, while other days it felt like it was overwhelming. The aura of pressure came in waves.

"You ready?" Savannah asked while leaning her back against the door, propping it open.

"Yes mom, now let's go look at this apartment."

Making our way out to the poorly lit hallway, Savannah strutted in front of me. She seemed excited and claimed we were going to a neighborhood we would all like.

I couldn't help but think that she picked this place on her own or possibly had Nicolette's assistance. Soon housing contracts would go out, and thanks to our student emails we couldn't forget. Reminders were going out left and right.

She pressed the down button, and to our luck the elevator came immediately.

"So what time are we supposed to meet her?"

"Two, I don't think it should take that long to get up there."

I highly doubted that. It was pushing 1:30 p.m. and we were headed to one of the neighborhoods that was the furthest north. We might as well be going to Evanston.

"Cool."

Making it out of the elevator, I looked around and no one I knew was there. With a small campus you were always bound to run into someone, and in my case, I was on high alert for Victor. I wasn't really sure where we were at the moment, sometimes we'd be on the best terms, and I'd hope we would bump into each other. The slightest miscommunication could put us in a Cold War. This all could be fixed with a short conversation but usually not without putting subliminal messages on our Snapchat stories for a week or two before one of us caved and asked to hang out without really addressing what made us stop talking in the first place.

If I wasn't dodging Victor, I was dodging his ex, Bria. Bria and I had a class together first semester and we were relatively friendly. We walked to class together twice and sided with each other in a few debates in Writing & Rhetoric. However, after I met Victor and found out she was his ex I made the decision to distance myself from her. I didn't want it to seem like I was breaking some sort of girl code rule. Technically, I didn't think that applied to me because we weren't really friends. Also is it even possible to steal someone's ex? I wasn't completely sure, but I tried to cut ties before it had the chance to get messy.

"I'm glad you guys finally made it down. We have to hurry up or we're going to be majorly late," Nicolette said while pushing through the lobby doors.

"What time is the next Brown Line train?"

"Twelve minutes," Savannah said while speed walking trying to keep up with Nicolette's pace.

I was there with them, but my mind was wandering off. *Why am I going to Ravenswood?* I thought to myself. *How did this even happen, why was I not even consulted?* I felt like I was being dragged along. Spring was doing its best to make an appearance, but winter was still trying to hold on. I was glad the sun decided to grace us with its presence.

Looking up I saw the moss green gargoyles atop of the Harold Washington Library, next to the Brown Line stop we were headed to. Walking the streets and gazing at architecture was just another reason I wasn't so ready to give up South Loop living.

"Come on Krista!" Nicolette yelled while looking back.

I was just a few steps behind them, Ravenswood was still going to be intact if we were a few minutes late. I wished they would relax a bit.

"I'm coming!" Picking up my pace slightly.

Breathing heavily and almost out of breath making it up each step to the train platform, I was not expecting to get a workout in this afternoon. My legs shook, and train tracks began to rattle as the train was making its way to our stop.

"This is Harold Washington Library, State & Van Buren," the automated, robotic voice announced and echoed throughout the air.

Nicolette and Savannah rushed toward the steel doors, waiting for them to open. I typically scanned each cart and opted for the emptiest one, but I didn't have the time to exercise my picky public transportation etiquette. The crowd rushed off and we pushed on.

"Doors closing. Adams & Wabash is next."

I chose a single seat that faced a window, these seats were a luxury most of the other "L" trains didn't have. Out of all the lines that you could take in the city, the Brown Line was the most peaceful. You could take a ride and bet on getting to your destination without being harassed for money, offered to buy single cigarettes, or serenaded by an off-key wannabe singer. Now if you wanted a show, just hop on the Red Line.

"So which stop is ours?" I faced both of them to confirm.

"I forgot, Savannah which one is it again?"

"We're getting off at Damen, guys."

"Oh my God, this is practically a field trip."

Nicolette giggled.

I couldn't be the only one who thought this was ridiculous. I didn't know much about real estate, but there had to be affordable living close to "our world." I whipped out my phone to confirm how many stops there were. My eyes enlarged. "Google Maps says that Damen is eighteen stops away," I emphasized *eighteen* so they can let that sink in.

"Damn Savannah, did you think this all the way through?" Nicolette asked.

"I can't believe the both of you are making such a big deal out of this."

"I'm sorry, I didn't really mean to but EIGHTEEN. Just think about it, this is going to be our commute every single day. That's a lot."

"No seriously, we already skip class living a few blocks away from campus, this would make us never want to go to class again," Nicolette chimed in.

This was an excellent point; it would get even worse with the slightest inconvenience like snow or me randomly letting one of my moods decide I just can't make it out of the bed that morning. We might as well drop out now.

"We haven't even given this place a chance, the realtor described the place as spacious and in a charming neighborhood," Savannah was doing the best she could to defend her choice.

"You're right, all this housing contract stuff just has me stressed out. Looking at the place couldn't hurt."

As Nicolette and Savannah kept droning on about apartments and next school year, my mind began to go somewhere else. The sound of the tracks underneath us began to mute, and their voices morphed into a muffled background noise. My ongoing thoughts transcended to the front of my mind, mostly fast, and jumbled. I no longer wanted to be here, so my mind decided I wouldn't.

"Merchandise Mart is next."

"That's where Krista wants to live."

Nicolette's joke made me smirk.

We were now only thirteen stops away.

Four million square feet, right on the river. The Merchandise Mart was practically a castle, and in my opinion resembled one. We were struggling with finding a place we could split three ways in rent, the thought of what it would take to acquire a building like that gave me a headache; if some miracle of mass proportions happened that would practically make me queen, and maybe Victor king?

I hadn't heard from him that weekend and wondered what he was up to. It was only the afternoon so I figured he couldn't have gotten into any trouble yet.

Looking out the window, I noticed the scenery change. Fewer skyscrapers and more well-manicured mini-lawns and newly-built brick multi-level homes. Fewer women in pencil skirts and tennis shoes maneuvering the sidewalks and more Lululemon clad moms strolling babies while jogging, Starbucks in one cup holder and tall bottled water in the other. We were definitely passing through Lincoln Park a.k.a Depaul country, as Nicolette, Savannah and I refer to it since Depaul

University's main campus was here. If you wanted a suburban and city mix this was the perfect spot for you.

In a way, Lincoln Park reminded me of home and I kind of liked it and hated it for that same reason.

I repositioned myself and took some pressure off my left butt cheek and placed more on the right, as my body signaled it was about to take a snooze. This was a ride I already wished was over. I could've sworn that it was announced that we just left Diversey, meaning eight more stops were left. If I was annoyed, I could only imagine how irritated Victor would be if he was going to leave campus to come visit me in the Ozarks.

Would he even make the trip? I couldn't picture him doing it. We already had our issues just a floor apart. If he did decide to make the trip he'd probably just complain about the whole thing. I could already hear him: "Why'd you pick to stay all the way up here," "You're gonna have to start coming downtown to see me," or whatever else I think Victor would say.

He might not mind. A piece of me hated how much I even considered his thoughts when we hadn't established anything worth me considering his commentary. I didn't even know what his housing plans were for next school year.

We hadn't taken the time to talk about it, and I'd been thinking about how to bring it up to him without sounding like I completely cared what his living decision was. On a scale of 1-10, I'd say I cared about a 6. I decided on 6 as it was slightly over halfway, so my feelings would only come off subtly higher than indifferent, leaning in the direction of actually caring. I think I took more time thinking about how I'd bring this up to him than putting thought into my actual plan for what I'd be doing, which is why my butt is asleep on a stale train chair on its way to Ravenswood. Maybe I should tone it down a bit, but anything Victor related intensified my overthinking nature.

How was sophomore year going to go when I still felt like I needed another semester just to get freshmen year right? Could Victor and I be for real next year? Could we find an apartment that actually made more sense?

"Damen is next," the automated announcement broke me out of my ongoing train of thought. I couldn't believe we were actually at the stop.

"See guys, this wasn't that bad," Savannah grinned and made her way toward the exit.

Getting off at Damen, my preconceived notions were confirmed. The closest thing in sight was a Mobil gas station, a vape shop, and a tattoo salon.

"The place is on Leland Ave," Savannah stated while staring down at her phone screen, trying to pinpoint our exact coordinates on her map.

"Ok, so then we just make a left and go up a block." Nicolette began leading the way, even though she was from Evanston, I thought she knew the city pretty well, especially the North side. As we turned, I saw a Thai place, a coffee shop, and a bike repair store a little further in the distance, its neon lights glistening from a far.

"We've got like five minutes," Savannah said as she click-clacked against the pavement at a high speed in her black, suede heeled booties.

Between her makeup and ensemble, I thought it was a bit much. I didn't find the need to try to impress the realtor, especially since we were in a neighborhood that was better suited for the type of person who was ready to settle down and were kind of over living in the city but didn't want to be completely away from everything. There were lots of dog walkers and homes that looked like they contained happy families with good credit. Also, the type of place that looked like if we decided to throw a rager, the cops would show up as if they were personally invited.

I matched their pace and tried to picture myself here. Maybe the Pristine Cup would be where I'd go grab a latte and become my go-grab-a-latte-and-go-to-study-spot after class. As far as the rest of my surroundings, I couldn't see indulging in whatever else the neighborhood had to offer. I couldn't believe we were already prepping for this step. In a way I was still getting used to waking up not seeing my mom and dad, arguing with Valentina over time in the bathroom, and making sure Kathryn didn't steal anything out of my closet. Now I'm here. That thought hits at the most random times like I didn't deliberately choose this city and it was forced upon me.

Me pretending to even be remotely invested in this misadventure was now draining the little energy I had reserved for this outing.

"This is it!" Savannah exclaimed with bright eyes and cheeks flushed with color from the nippy winds.

"It's definitely charming," I wasn't sure what to say, but I thought it was fitting enough for where we were.

It was much different from our high-rise, with yellow brick and only four stories high. The area was gated off, a courtyard in the center of all the units; the ivy-covered fountain in the middle of it all was a nice touch. Not exactly what I was expecting, and if I could stop the compare and contrast, I could actually like the space and enjoy where we were.

"Yoohoo! Ladies!"

We all turned around at the same time to see who could be trying to get our attention.

There was a woman with a jet black, choppy bob, and burgundy framed prescription glasses. Her plaid leggings and chiffon blouse clashed with her combat boots. I had no clue what she could possibly want with us.

"Hey girls, you're a little late but there's still enough time for me to show you around the place before my next appointment."

My eyes widened as I subtly scanned her from head to toe. I couldn't believe this frazzled looking woman was the realtor we were rushing to see.

"Cool, sorry for being late. Nice to meet you." Savannah extended her hand for a shake.

This woman struggled as she had a stack of file folders under one arm and a lipstick-stained Dunkin Donuts coffee cup in the other, switching it from her right hand to her left.

"Nice to meet you too. I'm Colleen and I'm looking forward to helping you find your next new place!"

"I'm Savannah, these are going to be my roommates, Nicolette and Krista."

I waved; Nicolette went for a handshake as well.

"So are you all coming from the south or west side?" she asked as she waddled toward the gate, trying to balance all that she was carrying.

My eyes squinted at this poorly put together woman who stepped out of an outdated, beat-up Acura. *Was she asking this because I'm Black, Nicolette was Mixed, and she thought Savannah was some White girl we found along our way to move to the north side with? Was she asking this because we were a few minutes late, and the only way to explain that would be the fact that we were coming from the south or west side?* Either way her micro-aggressive assumption settled right underneath my skin.

"The South Loop actually," I butted in like an ambassador on duty for my favorite neighborhood in the city.

"Oh wow! Nice, what brings you girls up this way?"

"Apparently this far north is cheap." My grin was there to passive aggressively represent that I am not to be played with, especially by a white woman who looked extremely underqualified to do her job.

Her once cheery demeanor drooped as her eyes peered into mine. Searching for a reason, I decided to respond as curt as I did. Savannah turned to look at me with an identical expression as Colleen's, I didn't care. Her commentary about us coming from the south or west side had to be addressed. I typically wouldn't have found the need to snap back or even know how to without sounding extremely offended. It was the mix of me not wanting to be here, this neighborhood's vibes, her drabby appearance, and her audacity to ask a stereotypically fueled question that allowed me to supply a perfect clap back.

The gate creaked as it slowly swung open to our possible future apartment, I was now entering the place more against it than I was coming in, which I didn't think was possible. I also got the urge to no longer be around Nicolette and Savannah for the rest of the day.

My phone buzzed.

I took it out of my pocket and smirked.

Victor: WYD?

I was trying to see him when this was over. A perfect distraction from this glitchy feeling hologram that I'd been transported to.

Me: Just hanging out with some friends

I didn't want to bring up the fact that we were looking at an apartment, especially since I didn't know what he was doing for housing yet. I felt like that would make things weird between us. Keeping it light was the best thing to do for now.

Victor: You have friends? JK. You should come by later though...

My eyes squinted, I reread the sentence, and my eyes zoomed in on the three dots in particular. Him adding the three dots annoyed me. *Why not straight up ask me to come over?* His being this casual prompted me to not respond right away and slid my phone back into my pocket.

"Ok so here is the courtyard, I think the fountain is a nice touch and adds some real character."

We all trailed behind her as she began her spiel. Making our way to the entrance of our building, I waited for that tingly feeling to kick in. It was the one I got in my spirit to confirm where I needed to be, to make sure this was my spot, my place, the one where I belonged. This feeling is something I looked for before I do anything new, it was the green light. I got that feeling with only a few things before, like touring my college. But instead, I was greeted with the smell of someone on the first floor heating up ramen.

Maybe I had a bad feeling about this for a reason outside of trying to keep the Chicago image I thought I should have, or it could also not be in God's plan for my life. I still had some time to figure that out, at least until the end of the tour. As we entered the building, the staircase was the first thing that caught my eye. The dark brown carpeting and oak banister looked like they winded on forever.

"So is there an elevator anywhere?" It was something I became used to, I don't think I could go without. I workout by choice, not by force.

"I'm afraid not, the unit is on the third floor. Hopefully that's not too much of a trek for ya."

After the commute and overall irritation, it felt like climbing a mountain.

"Not having an elevator won't be a problem," Savannah chimed in.

Maybe not for her, but for me, it was an addition to the con column on my mental pro and con list that my mind was formulating. With each step, I was trying to picture what the apartment would look like. Finally, we got to the front door, and Colleen was probably the only one who looked more excited than Savannah.

"Welcome to 3B!"

"This looks pretty good," Nicolette said unenthused. She stood in the middle of the living room; arms folded over her chest. Clad in beige carpet and empty eggshell walls, the shared living space was bigger than the living room we were currently in. So, there's one pro.

"Yeah, it's pretty nice," Savannah added.

Colleen turned to look at me. I had no comment.

"So, the place is 1,000 square feet and with rent being $1,850 that'll be ... a little over $600 split between the three of you."

Savannah's eyes gazed upward as if she could look into her brain, trying to calculate and see if this fit into her budget. Nicolette looked unphased by the statement. I had no clue what money was like back home these days due to the fact that my parents were still my personal sponsors. I knew that would be a talk where we would have to go into thorough details. I wasn't looking forward to that since anytime money was brought up over phone calls, there were long pauses or subject changes. Both were unhelpful as I felt in the dark about what was going on in the family and guilty about my unemployment status.

"Look around and get a feel for the place and let me know if you have any questions."

She stepped into the living room corner, giving us space to roam. Another pro I noticed was that this place had a large bay window. It was a nice touch even though there wasn't much to look at besides other buildings with a similar build as this one and cars lining the curb. Not exactly my style, but it did bring in beautiful natural light when the sun chose to grace us and make an appearance. I turned from the living room to make my way toward the kitchen we passed on the way in.

I stiffened. I felt like I had just witnessed a car accident.

"Are there any units with updated appliances?" I asked in disbelief at the white refrigerator and stove. Anything besides stainless steel was just a "No" for me.

"This is the most updated unit this building has available. The appliances are relatively new as well."

"It's just the fact that they're white. I prefer stainless steel."

"Okay, in the preferences form that was filled out the color of appliances wasn't highlighted."

I wasn't informed of a preference form, and everything about this place was screaming just that. I saw no trace of me in this mediocre walk-up. I walked out of the kitchen and passed the living room. I was pretty much completely over this apartment and officially over this realtor. Savannah and Nicolette had to be in one of those rooms.

"Krista, these rooms are pretty spacious," I heard Nicolette state as I passed the doorway.

I walked in, straight faced, and ready to express my disdain for this choice.

"Space is cool, but do you want to wake up and look at a brick wall every morning?" I pointed at her possible new bedroom window, which showed nothing but a reddish brick building that was directly next door.

"I don't think I care that much."

I leaned my head back and rolled my eyes. I felt alone in actually having some sort of lifestyle expectations. But a piece of me felt like there was no way in hell I could be the only one.

"Yeah, but you have a lotttt of stuff. Your sewing machine, rolls of fabric, damn near enough books to fill up a library, where would all of that stuff go?" I was hoping my questions would get the wheels turning in her head. Maybe she would get on my side to vote against this place.

"Hmmm... you're right. I didn't really think about that, just everything right now feels like a lot."

"I know, I can't believe we're actually looking at places off campus. It feels like just yesterday I moved there."

"Savannah was the main one really pushing this, I know living off campus saves money, but it just feels like more responsibility."

"Exactly, and this realtor looks like you can order her right off of Craigslist."

"Oh my gosh," Nicolette said through laughter.

"It's true, nothing about her or this place says, 'us.'"

"Honestly, I'm still not over the ride here, I cannot do that almost every day."

"I feel kind of bad for Savannah, I know she was excited about this place, but I just can't."

"There's other places, and we have some time to figure it out. I'm not really worried."

We left the room together. Savannah and Colleen were in the living room.

"Glad you guys could join us. What do you guys think of the place?" Colleen asked with a chipper tone.

I couldn't help but think that if this question was just addressed to me her voice would have less pep in it.

"I thought it was nice, just what we need," Savannah stated that like she was our assigned spokesperson. I was a bit floored but had no remaining energy to react. I would need every ounce left for our journey back.

"Nice. What did you ladies think?" Colleen addressed us both but was mostly making eye contact with Nicolette.

"The rooms were a nice size."

"Yes, there's enough room in all of these to at least fit a queen bed, dresser, and other decor comfortably."

"The bay window is cute," I had nothing else good to say, and was happy this tour was wrapping up. I thought throwing in at least one good comment was better than none, so it didn't look like I was dragging on the place the whole time.

"Ok, well if any of you have more questions about this property or would like to tour another that is up to everyone's standards, feel free to reach out." Colleen handed her card to Savannah only.

I was certain I was never coming to Ravenswood again: fluorescent lighting, one security guard shuffling through files on their desk while the other viewed security footage, the aroma of pepperoni, cheese, and marinara sauce coming from the pizza shop next door.

We were home and seeing a place that was so far from what I saw myself in ensured me that this was it. I now felt like it was my personal mission to keep it that way. Placing my pouch against the scanner next to the door that allowed access to the elevators, my fob turned the scanner green.

"Welcome back," one of the security guards said with his head behind the monitor.

Nicolette and Savannah followed me in. The clicking of Savannah's booties and the squeaking of our sneakers were more prominent than before since all of us were silent. No one uttered a word since we left the apartment in Ravenswood and departed from Colleen.

I didn't know what to say.

Sorry felt like the wrong thing to say because I couldn't apologize for not liking something. My stomach felt sunken and my palms felt damp; I felt the need to just throw something out there to break the silence. I was nervous due to the fact that I hated the place the most and Savannah could blame me for ruining the tour.

The elevator button light glared a bright orange as I pressed the arrow pointing upward.

"Maybe we can try another place next weekend," I offered as we boarded the elevator.

"We're running out of time though; we don't have the time to scour the city to find the most Instagram-worthy apartment that fits your vibe," Savannah growled, with her eyes glued to the glowing seventeenth floor button.

My brows furrowed, my right fist clenched, and I softly bit the left side of my cheek.

I thought she lost her mind; I was convinced Jesus was the only one helping me to keep my composure. My eyes glared at Nicolette, hopefully she would say something to help her friend out and diffuse the situation.

"Guy's let's just take a breather."

I glanced at the floor, disappointed with the fact that was the best she could come up with. In this situation, her overly relaxed approach was the least bit helpful.

"That's easy for you to say, you're not the one who's worried about money all of the time."

"That's not fair Savannah, I get you are but that doesn't mean we panic and take the first thing we find," Nicolette made the perfect point and delivered it much better than I would have in this circumstance.

I peeled my back off the wooden wall behind me facing the double doors, reached between the both of them to press sixteen. I couldn't get off this elevator fast enough.

Ding.

"I'll catch up with you guys later," I said squeezing between them, and making it off the elevator. The doors shut behind me, and I didn't hear them say anything back.

My heart pounded in my chest, a mix of frustration about our final housing outcome and anticipation of my visiting Victor. I was on edge. I paused in front of his door and whipped out my phone to use my front camera as a mirror. I tilted my head from the left to the right, trying to quickly analyze every little angle I've seen of my face for the last seventeen years. I wished I had put on a little makeup earlier since I was now here. I knocked three times, the sound echoing in the hallway.

"Who is it?"

"Krista."

"Who?"

"I hate you," I said turning on my heels on my way back to the elevator.

"I'm just playing! What took you so long?" Victor asked as his door made its way open.

"Long story," I sighed.

"With you, it always is." He made room for me to come in.

"What are you up to?"

"Just ordered a party pack."

I kicked my shoes in the foyer and placed my jacket on the knob of the hallway closet.

"Ordering drugs this early? I should've known you'd be up to no good."

I sat on the couch, and stared out the window for a bit, my heart eased its rapid pace.

"It could never be too early, plus I'm not doing anything later. I thought it'd be perfect for us to chill and have Kris & Victor time." He looked me right in my eyes.

When he did that, I always felt like he could see inside of me. Seeing me try to stop my brain from picturing our future together and seeing inner me coaching outer me to act cool.

"Well, you've got edibles in yours, right?"

"Of course, this isn't amateur hour."

"What flavor?"

"Fruity Pebble Rice Krispies."

"It'll do." It was actually perfect, but of course I wouldn't let him know that.

"So why didn't you text me back?" he asked while making his way over to the couch. He sat directly next to me, his legs touching mine. I wondered if he could feel the hair on my legs stand up through my pants.

"I'm sorry, I forgot." I folded my legs criss-cross and turned to face him.

"Mmm ... I don't believe it. You must've been with your other boyfriend," he speculated with his eyebrows raised.

I leaned my head to the right and rested it on my shoulder, wishing I could read his mind.

"Victor, Victor Victor ... always full of games."

"I've learned from the best, I never know what you're up to for real."

He had to be kidding me, I never knew game even remotely until I learned from him. I don't think he understood he was the teacher in this equation.

"You're not supposed to, especially since I could say the same about you."

There was a knock on the door. I jumped back a bit as I was surprised. My eyes shifted from the left and the right, looking for somewhere to possibly hide. *What if it was one of his many women paying him a surprise visit? Word would travel like wildfire.* A quick subtweet or a Snap and every student in the South Loop would know about this little gathering.

"Why do you look like you just saw a ghost? It's just our special delivery." He winked.

I felt like the room was centered again, released my legs from being tightly pulled to my chest and exhaled.

"Thanks man," Victor said while swapping two crumpled $20 bills for a plastic baggy.

"We can split the Rice Krispies but the rest is for me," he said as the door closed behind him.

"Someone else must've had a long day too."

"Try a long week princess. This housing stuff got me stressed out," he trailed off as he walked into the kitchen to slice our treat.

We were all feeling stressed at this moment. So much had taken place in the course of a few months. With me trying to find my way, create my path, and try on these different life suits; seeing which one would fit and when it didn't work anymore I'd shed that skin and blend in with what I thought worked. Wanting something, and then yearning to escape the space I designed was my new routine.

"Apparently I've got the time so you can tell me if you like." His lips thinned slightly, and the left side of his mouth curved; he should trust me with whatever he had to say by now. At least that's what I hoped. He turned the light off in the kitchen and walked back to the living room paper plate in hand topped with weed infused confetti colored goodness.

"I don't know where to start really, I guess everything."

"Care to elaborate?"

"How about we take these first, just don't eat your whole half at once. I feel like you might tweak."

"Oh my gosh, I'm not." Even though I believed I wouldn't I still only ate half of my piece just in case.

working

"Welcome to the Target crew, we're excited to bring you on board!" the head manager, Ted, proudly announced at the end of my last interview.

"I'm excited to be here!" I said while lying, doing my very best to mimic his authentic enthusiasm.

I was just happy I was about to start getting paid so I could start saving toward my school fund. This also meant no more conversations would be had about how my job search was going.

"We'll start your training in two days, pair you with a team lead, and see if you work better in our softlines or hardlines departments."

"Sounds good," I replied staring blankly back at him across the desk. After three rounds of interviews for a slightly above minimum wage job, my socially professional battery was running low, and I was ready to leave this stuffy office and go back home.

"Alright, we'll email your upcoming schedule. If you have any questions in the meantime don't hesitate to reach out."

"Will do, thanks again for this opportunity," I said while I extended my hand for a handshake.

"You're welcome," Ted replied as he stood up and met my hand with his.

Walking out of the building, I didn't really know how I felt. Knowing this was my best employment option was discouraging to whom I really saw myself as, not the way the world sees me now. They had no clue about all the ideas that lived inside me, but now was not the time and Target was not the place for them. The mall or some other fast-food establishment around wasn't either.

"I got the job," I announced to my mom as I got in the passenger seat of her car.

"That's amazing!" she exclaimed.

She was definitely more excited than I. The job wasn't *amazing*. I think she meant more of the fact that there was a light at the end of the tunnel. Honestly, it did give my tense body an overwhelming sense of relief. I may become the best curator from the Midwest, but I had to graduate first. Target was a part of my path to get there in my case. I had about ten weeks to make $2,129.82, and forty hours a week. I knew I could do it. No matter how gruesome it felt.

I had been working at Target for two weeks, and had eight weeks left to go.

Going through training was a breeze. I tried to explain that I knew how to work in a store, and I knew how to use pricing tools, but my team lead was adamant that I knew how to do it the "Target way."

"These are our MyDevices. You can use these to scan barcodes for the price and to see if the item is in stock at this location or at another location."

"Cool," I said because I didn't really know what to say. He explained it with such joy I wanted to reciprocate some interest.

"They're the most advanced pricing tools of their kind, no other store has one quite like it."

"Wow, that's cool." I thought that was a step up from just cool and made it look like I had some genuine interest. That was the least I could do, because I wasn't interested at all, but I didn't want to hurt his feelings.

"So, tell me about yourself," he said, dying to change the conversation.

I paused for a moment. I didn't really know what to say, especially because he was one of my managers. I knew it had to be personal, but clearly not anything that I would tell a best friend.

"I don't know what to say."

"Come on, there has to be something," he said with a giggle.

"Well, I love art. I have an appreciation for all forms but going to gallery openings and seeing an artist's vision come together is my favorite. I love eating, I could probably eat all day, and I love God."

He was quiet for a moment. I know he felt uncomfortable about me bringing up God but I couldn't hold that back. God has been more prevalent in my life lately. I had been praying to Him more because this mission to get the most money I'd ever seen in my personal checking account was testing my faith. I couldn't leave Him out of the "tell me about yourself" answer, I wouldn't have felt right.

"So, tell me about *your*self?" I asked to break the awkward silence.

"*Ummm* ... When I'm not here I'm working out, with my wife and kids, and rarely doing anything else. Sometimes I get excited when I pitch a new idea to upper management, but that's about it."

I thought that was the saddest thing I had ever heard. I tried my best not to pass any judgements, because I'm just human, and eighteen with nothing to my name. But I couldn't have gotten a clearer picture of what I didn't want my life to look like.

I never would've guessed that working for Target would've been so serious. I had no clue during my application process that I was applying for a job as matter-of-fact as the CIA. My manager explained to me the way employees should carry themselves once they hit the sales floor, in our uniforms we were sup-posed to take pride in wearing. We had to be super-fast, while being super-friendly, communicate on our walk-ies, and respond for back-up whenever a team member needed help.

Great, I thought to myself. Not only is this like working for the Central Intelligence Agency but I am also supposed to be Superman too.

I thought that was full of crap, but of course I didn't say anything. I just let the guy drone on about the Target principles as he gave me a tour of the place; he knew it like it was the back of his hand. Even though I was irritated at the time I noticed how ecstatic he was while he talked, and it surprised me because it seemed genuine. It more than likely was, I just didn't under-stand why he would be enthused about working here. I began to wonder how long he had worked here; did he want to continue climbing up the Target food chain and become an even bigger manager with some cool, significant sounding title like "top executive manager" or did he have higher aspirations? These were things I was naturally curious about but wasn't going to ask. I didn't know how to word it without sounding like a snob. It was just one of those things I couldn't help but think about.

"So, all merchandise that is sold on the tile is con-sidered our hardlines department, and everything sold on the carpet is softlines."

"That's actually pretty clever," was my genuine response.

"Right? I thought so too!" he beamed as I showed some intrigue.

"Besides that, is there any other difference?"

"I'm glad you asked, let's go into this aisle for a second so I can show you."

We were now standing in front of cleaning supplies, it all looked up to par to me.

"At first glance, do you see anything that could be improved?"

I looked around for a second, nothing was out of place, every item matched perfectly with other items with the same brand. This felt like a trick question.

"Not that I can tell," I answered apprehensively.

"Not many can, but if you notice some of the products are pushed back and the diamonds on the racks are showing. The goal is to keep the diamonds covered at all times."

"Ok, but why?" I would've never guessed this was an actual thing if Mark weren't here right now explaining this to me. You could literally spend all day pushing things forward due to how much traffic these aisles see.

"At Target, we want each aisle to look like the customers' first time here, it enhances the shoppers' experience."

"Gotcha."

"Mark, come in. We're backed up on register 9. Mark, come in. We're backed up on register 9," his walkie talkie blared from the side of his belt buckle.

"I'll be right there," he responded.

"Let's just have you work on aisle A9-A20 until the end of your shift."

"Ok," I said as he rushed to register 9.

I began to push forward bottles of Fabuloso and multi-surface cleaner. One by one, mindlessly, but still ensuring the diamonds were covered, hoping that no one would walk through and ruin this set up, and that the end of my shift would hurry up.

"Just eight more weeks of this," I mumbled to myself.

After my four-week stint in hardlines, they finally let me outside of Mark's shadow and sent me to test drive the softlines department. It was three middle-aged women who looked like they could've been born here. They had their system in which I felt like I was imposing on instead of becoming an asset to. One worked maintaining the clothes on the sales floor, one manned the fitting rooms, and the other worked in shoes.

"Hey ladies, I wanted to introduce you to Krista. She's a new employee and has been working in hard-lines but we wanted to see how she did in softlines," Katy introduced me to them like a game show host.

They look unimpressed to say the least.

"Nice to meet everyone," I added to just break the silence.

They responded with more blank stares, and now I missed the silence and solitude of pushing products forward on shelves.

"I know you all can make her feel welcome. I'm confident that I'm leaving her with people who can show her the ropes," Katy ensured.

I thought she might have lost her mind in one of the aisles on the way over here. She must not have been in front of the same ladies I was. The ladies were gatekeeping this section of the store like it was their birthright.

"Nice to have you, Krista," the one in charge of the dressing room stated flatly.

"I'll be back here in a few hours to check on how things are going," Katy said as she bounced away.

I felt like she left me with the wolves. I just need two more checks, and I'll be back to my real life. I don't think these oldies could be that bad, at least I hoped they couldn't.

"So, what are the main rules for softlines?" I asked just to get straight to why I was here, which was work.

"It's simple actually. Fold, organize, and make sure no one steals. I only do two of those things though, no one pays me enough to care if somebody is stealing. My name is Martha by the way."

I refrained from cackling.

"Martha, it's her first day over here; you don't need to scare her off. We don't know her yet; she could tell Katy on us. Nice to meet you Krista. I'm Alisha."

I was trying to not act confused as they were hanging up clothes. *Where was all this coming from?*

"I'm Drena, don't mind how we acted a few minutes ago. We cannot stand Katy. She's like a mosquito that buzzes around this place, simply annoying as hell."

I wouldn't necessarily disagree, but I wouldn't be here long enough for her to get under my skin as much.

Getting to know Martha, Alisha, and Drena was my favorite part of coming to work. I actually began to open up to them about the real me.

"So, this Victor guy you speak of rubs me the wrong way," Martha explained as we were folding the breathable summer tees.

"How so?" I inquired out of pure intrigue. Now that Valentina was gone, I never spoke out loud about him to anyone. I needed some much older, wiser insight.

"Ok he likes you, but what? Why hasn't he asked you to be his girlfriend? You're the definition of a catch, and he's just a knucklehead."

I totally agreed with her statement. Us liking each other seemed like it was getting us nowhere fast, and I hadn't talked to him in weeks. Some of this was due to being laser focused on finding a job, interview prep, and training here. The other part was due to the mixed signals, a girl can only take so many of those. Ironically, my phone hadn't rung either so that meant he was busy doing him.

"I agree with the knucklehead part, but knowing I'm going to see him in a few weeks doesn't make any of this easy."

"Girl, if I was your age living in a big city like Chicago, he would be the very last thing on my mind. But things are so different than they were in my day. I would be concentrating on school while going out with 100 Victors," Martha encouraged as she looked off in the distance, simultaneously folding shirts.

Her words replayed in my mind as I color-coded the tees and made sure they were in order from XS to XXL.

"You're right," I sighed.

As more time went on, I thought about what their dreams were, especially on days when they walked in with long faces resembling mules.

"How are you today, Drena?" I asked happily to the fitting room attendant as she drearily trudged her way over to her station. My time was dwindling here, and my dad confirmed he sent half of the money to my school. I didn't have a single reason to feel anything but pure joy.

"Oh, I'm just making it. How are you?"

"I'm doing good, and what do you mean by 'just making it'?"

"I'm just getting by; I don't want to be here but I'm still alive so I shouldn't have any complaints," she said in a monotone voice.

"Well, I hope this day is better," I hated it when I didn't know what to say.

"Thank you, that's very sweet of you."

I walked away and went to the men's jeans table to start folding and thought that was now the saddest thing I've ever heard. At this place it was always a saying from a crew member that outdid the saddest thing I ever heard prior to the one before.

This couldn't be it for them, and I wondered if they were even working toward whatever it was they wanted. When I thought these things, I would pray for them all. Even if I wasn't around long enough to see the results of my prayers, I knew God was listening and would help them in the best way He saw fit for them.

As my time at Target continued, I made sure I was friendly toward everyone I worked with, but not too friendly where they thought I would actually want to be friends. I would flash a toothless grin to anyone who was wearing a red polo and khaki pants, or wave to them in passing. I was never the one to ask how someone's weekend went, show up to staff bowling nights, or take my breaks with other people. "Stack my chips and dip" was the motto I kept on repeating in my head. Sometimes it felt like I said it so loudly I thought everyone else around me heard me. I just wanted to clock-in and clock-out.

I wasn't buddy-buddy with my co-workers, except for my "softlines sisters." Martha came up with the name, and surprisingly it grew on me. Even more surprising than that, my managers took a liking to me. I always got compliments on how I always stayed on task, got thanked for coming in on time, and they appreciated the fact I didn't try to be slick and extend my half-hour break to an hour to have loud conversations or friendly debates in the break room with other employees like everyone else did. I was never goofing off or trying to flirt with anyone, which was another thing almost everyone else did. I didn't have anybody to do these things with; I had absolutely zero interest in anyone there.

"Good job on rearranging the men's clearance swimming trunks Krista, it's always such a mess!" Katy cheerfully expressed.

"Thank you!" I said while hanging up some of the sweaters that just arrived.

"I'm going to be sad to see you go, I don't know if anyone can get that section together quite like you."

"I'm sure you guys will manage," I said with a smile. I always tried to match Katy's peppiness every time we talked. I had put in my two-week notice two days ago, and everything felt so much more real to me. I was going back to school, and to hear Katy kid me about wasting my life away just to keep a section tidy showcased how brainwashed anyone with the title "lead" was here. This was their life, more than their bread and butter, but it was like it was ingrained in them. I'm not sure how much they were getting paid, but no check could get me to act like that. I could see why most of my coworkers hated her because they thought her attitude was fake.

"Katy is always bouncing around the store, it's so annoying," I overheard another employee say to someone else.

"I know, I think she's on drugs or something."

"Exactly, there is no way in hell someone could be that happy all the time."

"She could be getting laid a lot, you know I heard she's been hooking up with another manager."

"No way! Who?"

"I don't know, but when I find out I'll let you know."

Being happy here wasn't a thing, the only way to fit or be well-liked here was to be negative and gloomy like everyone else or to be dating another employee. Or in my case it was because I know I'm about to be leaving for good.

Even though a few guys tried to distract me, only one asked me on a date, but I knew it could never work. Besides me leaving and being dead set on starting my life over, he was too into his job here and was overly outgoing. I believe in taking pride in your work; it just disturbed me he put so much pride into working here. I mean, what if things went great between us and we ended up together, and I was one of the most successful gallery owners where I lived, and he worked at Target. That would just be terrible. I would also consider myself outgoing, but he took it to an extreme level. My outgoingness reached the height of this building, while his reached the height of the Burj Khalifa in Dubai.

"Hi Krista! How are you today? Trent asked me loudly at 8 a.m. on a Saturday.

"I'm doing fine," I said while rubbing my eyes and putting my lunch in my locker.

"You're looking fine, but you should be feeling great now that you're at Target."

Oh Lord, I thought. That was easily the worst pick up line I had ever heard and I wondered why he was saying this, there weren't any managers around and I'm pretty sure he wasn't getting paid extra to be a Target sponsor.

"Thanks, and I'll feel better soon, I'm just tired." I wish I never said thanks to his attempt to flirting with me, not to be rude but because I had zero percent interest in going out with Target's mascot.

"So do you have this weekend off?"

At this very moment I wanted to ascend to Heaven and get out of this conversation. I already knew where this was leading, he was definitely about to ask me out. I didn't want to lie, and I didn't want to make myself uncomfortable and take him up on his offer of going out with him.

"I believe I'm off, but if I am I'll probably be busy with family stuff."

"Well, if you're not busy with family stuff do you want to go see a movie with me and grab something to eat?"

"Maybe, I'll let you know." Even though I really wanted to say no, I didn't have the heart to do it and I didn't want to hurt his feelings.

After that conversation I avoided him until my last day of work. Anytime I thought I saw him out of the corner of my eye I would go the opposite way, when I heard him announce he was going on his break on the walkie I would wait even longer to go on mine. Every time I exited the building, I wouldn't even glance toward the cash register he worked on, in fear we would make eye contact.

So much for being cool and sophisticated.

Then there was one guy who I thought was remotely cute, but he never talked to me. He always stared at me and every time he was having a conversation with someone, and I came around he would stop talking. I didn't have the time or energy to play into any of it.

Having good relationships with my bosses was nice, though. They never treated me like a kid, talked down to me, or were aggressive just because they were the ones in charge. It was such a beautiful change from my last job. In return, I never felt the need to rebel against them. They were now people I could add to my list of references for the next place I applied to. Hopefully, that job would be more permanent than this, and somewhere I would be proud to say I worked. It would be nice to work at a place for more than a month or a school year for a change.

Today was the last day of work during my second to last week of work. It was currently 4:45 p.m. and I was scheduled to go on break at 5:00 p.m. My section looked very well-kept. By the time I found my groove in the softlines department, I always picked to work in the men's clothing section, because it was the easiest to manage. It never got messy like the women's or kids' section.

Those two sections always appeared like they were rummaged through by wild animals. Clothes were always strewn about the floor, and there was always a glitter mishap in the kids' section because that's what practically every article of clothing was made with. Don't let me get started on the shoe section, it was always a nightmare. I never thought it would be such a hard task for people to put things back where they got them from, but I guess it was because it never happened. Please don't let it be a sale going on, I would usually hear employees curse under their breath about how much they hated their jobs and messy shoppers.

Men shoppers usually came in to get their item or two without acknowledging my existence and they were off to the register. They didn't even try things on, they just grabbed it and left. I had no complaints; they made my job easier. I usually refolded everything I'd already folded and put the hangers in order from the smallest size to the largest, and I couldn't forget to make sure the hangers were finger width apart or the world might have ended. That's exactly what I was doing now to pass these filler minutes before my break. Filler minutes were just something I referred to as time I was trying to kill while I waited for something else to happen; and something I found myself doing too often.

Actually, this whole summer felt like filler minutes, between work, going home, and not being able to spend the money I made, there was nothing to do. I was overdue for a party, I could already imagine the first weekend back on campus, which made me want to just fast forward to that part already.

I refolded the polos, v-neck tees, crew neck tees, and every other tee imaginable. I checked my surroundings to make sure a boss or employee wasn't around before I grabbed my phone out of my pocket to check the time. It was 4:59 p.m. It was now the time for me to announce over the walkies that I hated so much that I was going on my break. I hated the walkies because we had to announce our every move on them. I enjoyed feeling like I was off in my own world folding clothes without being bothered. That was impossible to do with a manager asking, "What's your location?" every fifteen minutes or so. I also hated hearing someone talk on them every few minutes because their voices would clash while a customer talked to me; it was beyond annoying.

I walked to the frozen food section to see what I wanted to eat on my break. I stood in front of the freezers and stared at the fogged glass doors. I was trying to decide what Lean Cuisine I wanted. There were so many choices which always made it difficult. But I knew I would end up picking between a pizza or panini. Narrowing the choices down to two was never the hard part for me, it was always choosing between the two. I factored in which one had more calories, which one looked the best on the outside of the box, and I've had almost every pizza so I knew how they tasted so sometimes I wanted to try something new and I would go with the panini. Then I would think, *What if I don't like the panini? I should just stick with the pizza.* Then I would think, *How bad can a panini actually end up tasting?* For a second, I wondered if anyone else took so much time to make their frozen food selections. I looked around and everyone just grabbed their items and rolled their carts down the aisle.

I opened the freezer, and the aroma of frozen pepperoni filled my nose as I leaned in and grabbed the panini. This wasn't a life-altering decision I was making, it was just what I was going to eat during my break at work. Even though I knew this wasn't a big deal, as I walked out of the frozen food aisle, I couldn't help but to feel like I was missing out on a pizza I had already tasted before.

I got up to the register and paid for my meal. When asked if I wanted to use my employee discount I said no, because I always forgot my discount card at home, and I didn't see the point of using it anyway. It only gave me 10% off my entire purchase; I wouldn't consider that to be an employee perk.

These were the types of things that made me anticipate being in charge of something. I wanted my employees to feel appreciated and get perks that actually made them happy, like vacations for being a good employee or having a staff rewards program. Maybe my ideas were too large scale for Target, but at least a 50% employee discount would have been nice. I thought I could put that in the suggestion box before I left. I'm sure everyone would enjoy that more than a new couch in the break room that would end up getting just as worn out as the one already there or changing the playlist that had soft 90s rock songs stuck in my head.

The breakroom was depressing; the fluorescent lights flickered, the tattered chocolate brown leather sofa wedged in a corner, a table with a microwave probably as old as me, and a few fold-out chairs sat in front of the out-of-date TV that had few to no channels. It wasn't exactly Heaven on Earth, but it was a break from being on Hell's floor.

reminiscing

It was seventy-seven degrees, sunny, and no humidity. Today was my day off from work, and in my eyes the weather was perfect, so I decided to walk back to the riverbank.

I sat down on the same bench, the ducks were in their same spot, and there was no one else around. I wondered if anyone came here, it wasn't the most scenic place on the planet, it didn't have a gorgeous view of the Chicago skyline, but it was serene, and I thought it had character. I appreciated its silence and the calmness it provided me with. I needed that right now because the school year was about to start, and I was anxious. I knew I wouldn't be able to have many moments like this once the school year started. This spot gave me peace. This was something the city with all its glitzy perks could never provide me with.

"It should be a breeze," I kept saying to myself repeatedly out loud. I knew deep down everything would be fine, but I always worried anyway because of the fear of unknown possibilities life throws my way. I was no longer a freshman who didn't know where her classes were. I didn't have to feel obligated to go to every social gathering the school held to force people to make friends. I wasn't going to have an RA knocking on my door to check up on how my college experience was going.

I was now going to be a sophisticated sophomore, or at least that's what I thought I would be. I would know my way around the city, and I was no longer afraid of taking an Uber. At first, I thought it was the strangest thing ever. I thought, *Why would I want to get in a car with someone I don't even know,* but as the year progressed my fear of them completely vanished. I figured they came in handy, especially taking my drunk friends and me back to the dorms on weekend nights. I would now be the student who answered people's questions instead of the one asking all of them. I thought the best part of this year is that I won't have any random roommates.

Savannah, Nicolette, and I decided to room together, and stay on campus. We came to a collective agreement that it would be the best for us. Savannah was one of my roommates last year, and we got along the best. That didn't mean that much though because I wasn't close with other girls. Nicolette was Savannah's friend, and they met their freshman year. One day during my freshman year, I remember coming from class seeing Nicolette on our couch with Savannah; I said, "Hi," because I thought it was the nice thing to do. I didn't think she would be back or show up much because I'd talked to many people my roommates had over and they never came back. I thought she'd be one of those people too, but day after day I would come back from class, and she was there sitting in the same spot on the couch. So, one day after class I decided to join in on their conversation.

"Hey, what's your name?"

"Nicolette, what's yours?"

"Krista."

"What do you think Savannah should do with her designs? I think she should submit them into the school's design of the week competition," Nicolette exclaimed.

I honestly didn't have an answer to that. I never saw her work on anything before, I knew she was a fashion major, but I never saw the work she created.

"I don't know, but it wouldn't hurt to give it a shot."

"I was thinking about it, but I don't know, I don't think it will get picked."

"Why don't you just try it and see," I said trying to encourage Savannah.

"Yeah, you never know what could happen," Nicolette echoed.

"You guys are right. I'll think about it."

Nicolette and I glanced at each other for a moment. We both knew her "thinking about it" was going to result in her not doing it.

After that day, I started talking with them every day, and we just melded as friends.

Nicolette was just the type of person you could do that with. She loved meeting new people and could spark a conversation with anyone no matter if we were in the elevator with other people or in a line at Starbucks.

"Oh my gosh! Your dog is so cute!" Nicolette shouted.

All three of us were on an elevator with some guy who didn't go to school but just lived in the building. Sometimes I wondered if this type of thing happened because I went to an urban art school or would this be a thing if I went through with being a Michigan State Spartan.

"Why thank you, his name is Charles," he said smiling as if the reason his dog was cute was because he was his owner.

"That's so cute, and I love you guys having matching sweaters."

I personally thought they were obnoxious, so I said nothing. Plus, I was never the type of girl to go crazy when a dog came around. Savannah just watched the conversation take place without saying a word.

"Thank you, I thought they were just adorable! They were also on sale so I couldn't resist them!"

"Maybe I could bring my dogs from home one day so they could have a playdate."

"That would be lovely. I think Charles gets lonely when I don't have the energy to play with him."

The elevator door opened, and he made his way off.

"Nice meeting you young lady, Charles and I will be looking forward to that playdate."

"Ok!"

I wondered if she was serious, but I didn't ask her. I knew it was just elevator chatter.

I loved that about her, it was something I could never do, and she did it so effortlessly. She wasn't cliquey at all which made her different from other fashion students I met. She cracked jokes all the time, mostly inappropriate humor but everyone enjoyed it, nonetheless. She was the life of the party and was the reason Savannah and I knew about any.

I fit nicely with both of them. I laughed at almost everything, I was the one to never take things too seriously. With them I didn't have to play the same role I did at home. I didn't have the weight of my parents or how people viewed me in the past looming over me. Out of the three of us, I was the most optimistic. I always weighed out all our options, usually it was just for things like who was going to supply us with liquor for the weekend and when I was able to come through and provide it, I felt special. Like it was showing that even though I was the youngest out of all of us I was "cool." I think I was just trying to prove I was cool to myself. I wished Valentina could see me, I think she would've even been impressed.

I also was the only one out of the three of us who wasn't a fashion major, so I provided good feedback from a consumer point of view. When there was tension in the room from creative disagreements while they were working on projects, I was the peacemaker. Savannah's style was skater streetwear meets femininity while Nicolette's creations were straight up hip-hop inspired. They both had good ideas, but they were better off working separately. It was also good for me not to hear a passive aggressive argument and having to break it up by saying things like "Let's all agree to disagree," or "If no one has anything nice to say don't say anything at all."

We all just went together well, and when it was time for housing contracts to be filled out, we all agreed it just made sense for us to room together.

I was even planning to be more focused than I was last school year. My first semester, I was focused and even ahead in some of my classes. I felt like I didn't have a choice to not do well academically; it wasn't like I had an overflowing social calendar to attend to. Second semester came and everything changed, in fact they felt like two completely different school years.

The first eight weekends of the second semester were all jumbled in my mind. It was a mashup of parties where I met new people and barely remembered anything the next day or going to a party in the wrong neighborhood and running out with a crowd of people because a fight was about to break out. I remember that party vividly because I was sober during the whole thing. Nicolette suggested we go, but she failed to mention it was a stoner party and none of us smoked regularly. During the whole thing I was thinking, *Where is the liquor?* while I circled the whole room hoping a bottle would appear.

The apartment was small and dark, some type of drill music was playing in the background. As I was walking around and maneuvering my head to see if I could peep a bottle of anything I noticed a group of dreadheads who all literally could enter a Chief Keef look-a-like competition, were huddled in the kitchen and staring at me. I tried not to make eye contact. Eye contact was an automatic invitation for conversation. The thing was, my best bet for obtaining liquor would be getting it in the kitchen.

"*Uhh ...*" I sighed aloud. *The things we have to go through to have a good time,* I said in my head.

As I made my way over, they all smiled. I was scared but I smiled back.

"You cute as hell," I heard one of them say loudly over the loud music.

"Thanks," I yelled back.

The conversation ended just as quickly as it started as soon as we heard someone whoosh open a door very quickly and it slammed even quicker than it was opened adjacent from the kitchen.

"Man, what the hell are you doing?" I heard someone yell.

There were certain doors, you just don't open at parties and clearly this guy didn't know that.

Then there was a loud bang; I am almost sure it was a gunshot. My conclusion had to be correct because even the people pasted to the sofa smoking weed were quick to their feet. Everyone was pushing and shoving to get out of there.

The funniest part about that night was while running out of the party I noticed one of the guys who was there casually walked as if none of this phased him. He clearly was from around there, and by the looks of the area I'm sure this happened all the time. We made it out of the house and got a few blocks down and Nicolette was panicking trying to get us an Uber.

"Oh my gosh we're going to die!" Nicolette managed to say while crying and running.

"It was your whole idea to come out here!" Savannah said.

I'm thinking both of these statements were pointless as we were running with a sea of people trying to find safety. I'm also wishing I never came along for this one.

"Why don't we just go over there and order an Uber," I said pointing at a hot dog joint.

We stood under the awning shivering, but were finally a few blocks away from the chaos. This spot felt like the safe zone even though we were still clearly in the hood.

"I can't even type, my fingers are so damn cold," Nicolette growled as she typed in our location.

"I really hope this guy hurries, I don't want to die here tonight," Savannah said on the brink of tears.

I wanted to scream, "Shut the hell up! We are not going to die!" but no words managed to leave my mouth.

I felt dazed. I felt like what I was experiencing wasn't real, like it was a movie. I was the star, the viewer, and narrating the entire thing in my mind. I thought if this was my first semester, I would be eating snacks and watching Netflix, or waiting for Victor to hit me up to chill in his room. I suddenly wanted my cozy first semester life back. This was more than I had bargained for.

While we were huddled together on the sidewalk waiting for our rescue the same guy casually walking out the party like he was strolling through Millennium Park on a Sunday afternoon approached us. I had no clue what was about to come out of his mouth but now I wasn't feeling dazed, I was scared. I thought about the fact I could've died right there on West 47th Street; it would've all been for a party I didn't even enjoy. I knew at the very moment something had to change; I couldn't continue on like this.

To my surprise he said, "Do you guys want this bottle of Henny, since the party is over, I don't need it anymore."

We were all quiet and apprehensive. A strange man just wanted to give us an unopened bottle of Hennessy, we all felt like it was too good to be true. I also wondered why I didn't run into him while I was hunting for it in the party.

"Sure!" Nicolette said excitedly, her whole scared demeanor dropped as he handed over the bottle to her.

"Thank you," I said slowly not fully believing how I went from running out of a party, from fearing losing my life, to getting a free bottle of cognac.

"You're welcome, ladies," he said as he walked off.

I watched him walk away and thought anything can happen in the city. I loved Chicago for making me feel that way. This wouldn't have happened to me back home.

We all took a swig and squealed as we saw our Uber driver arrive.

Most of these drunken, hazy nights ended with us eating crappy but good tasting fast-food and Nicolette giving the drive-thru operator a hard time, while Savannah and I cackled like hyenas in the background.

"Can I get three double cheeseburgers!?" Nicolette screamed ordering for all three of us.

"*Uhhh* ... can I get you anything else with that?" the girl asked annoyed we chose to interrupt her shift with our drunken behavior.

Nicolette, Savannah, and I looked at each other and scrunched our faces not approving her attitude.

"Yeah! Actually, you can suck my ass!"

I just hoped our food didn't get spat on.

When we would make it back to the dorm, I would fall asleep on our couch, but always managed to wake up early enough to go to church on Sunday morning.

Nicolette and Savannah would make fun of me, but that was my tradition.

"Krista what the hell is wrong with you?" Nicolette asked.

"What do you mean?"

"It's like you're two different people."

"Yeah, Nicolette is right," Savannah chimed in.

I paused to think. Even though I was getting pissed because she brought this up; she had a good point.

"You can't be on fire for Jesus one moment and easily blend in with those who don't know or have no interest of knowing who He is," Nicolette went on.

That's how they saw it, I didn't see it that way though. It was more like I went to church to learn about life and what to do while I was here.

"I love Jesus, and I love a good party every now and then. Plus, I'm never the one to get sloppy drunk or tell people to, "Suck my ass." I believe He even watches over me as we get ourselves into the predicaments that we do. I'm young as hell what do you expect me to do; rot in the dorm during my free time?"

"Whatever, Krista," Savannah said while rolling her eyes.

Whatever was right, to me I just made it plain and would never have to explain this to them again.

They didn't understand and I didn't expect them to. I grew up with Him because He was presented to me. He chose me, and I chose Him back. I accepted Him as my personal Saviour when I was five, I never knew how much I needed Him until I left home and became a citizen of the "real world." One day I hope they would come to church with me and they would understand it for themselves, and one day I would be brave enough to invite them.

But what they didn't know and didn't understand was what He did. I felt it was only right to put God in the mix of all this craziness. The partying felt like a relief from the school week, and a break from always thinking about Victor. I thought this was a way for me to choose a life for myself apart from him. I thought the alcohol would provide some type of solace from my overactive mind, but it only made it race more. In all honesty, it was just something to do, and no one could make me feel bad about my decisions because I genuinely didn't feel as if I was doing anything wrong.

Going to church on Sunday and receiving the word of God provided consolation for all of it. Then the weekly cycle would start all over again. I was caught in the middle of my lifestyle choices. I thought I could balance this plus school. At first, I wondered how God felt about all of this, and deep down I didn't know if he approved. I wasn't supposed to add God into the mix, as if He were a missing ingredient to a soup recipe. He was supposed to be put as the head of my life and be treated as if I couldn't live without Him.

Being here at this moment, water wading, quacks echoing in the distance I remembered one of my walks to Lake Michigan with Victor.

"I wasn't even a good boyfriend to Bria," Victor said plainly, no shame, no regret; just like it was a fact, like stating the sky was blue.

I had heard the rumors, but I wanted to hear it from him. It took a very strong stomach for this type of thing, not one I knew I had until I met him.

"Why?"

"I don't know, it's hard to explain."

"Could you try?"

We locked eyes for a moment, studying each other's pupils. In this moment I wished I could read his mind, only then I could I fully trust the words that came out of his mouth. Here he could draw closer to himself and dismiss my question with a generalized statement, I hoped he'd reveal another layer of himself.

"Well, we just got together. We had met at one of those freshman events before classes actually started. I didn't really want to, but it was a guarantee I'd have someone to hook up with just in case I couldn't bag as many girls as I'd hope to."

"I can't believe I asked for this."

"You seem to get what you want princess." He said in the most condescending tone he's ever taken with me.

I saw him though, not surprised but I got everything I needed straight from the source instead of muffled whispers and contorted details from the rest of the student body who thought they knew something or wanted so desperately to be a part of the mix.

"So how did this end?"

"She cheated on me while we were on a break, with some guy from U of I around Halloween."

"How'd you feel?"

"I didn't really care."

"Really?" I had a hard time believing that. *How could someone not care about getting cheated on?* I knew I wasn't a relationship expert but I'm more than sure that's not how that goes.

"Yeah really," he giggled. "You can't really care if you don't care about the person. We both just wanted to know what it was like to do each other so we just did each other."

"This conversation is now over."

"This is why girls shouldn't ask questions they aren't prepared to get real answers to."

"Well thank you for preparing me with the worst. I don't think anything I'll hear after that could possibly compare. You have set the tone."

Now over everything that this conversation had brought on, I was ready to get into anything that could possibly distract me from the fact that I could very well be in love with a man who had no soul.

"But who else would you have these conversations with?" he asked with his left eyebrow raised.

This was a question I did not have an answer to. I never thought I'd have these conversations at all, I didn't think they existed. *Did other couples talk about things like this, or in our case not-couples?* I wonder if my parents did or anyone else who had been able to weather a long-standing relationship with someone else. *Did these conversations shorten the relationship since honesty and the raw, gut-wrenching kind could be too much for them? Or did they bring you closer together if the piercing words didn't slice right through you?* Another thing I didn't have an answer to.

"You want to do something fun?" I asked, now being bored of just chilling in his room.

"Like what?"

"We could walk to the lake."

He looked around for a moment, both hands on his hips debating if that would be his idea of fun.

"You know what Krista, sure let's walk to the lake," he said in his "proper voice," the one he uses to mimic me even though he exaggerates it to the point he sounds like a middle-aged white male game show host or sometimes he does it where he could have a starring role as a character on *The Hills* or *The Simple Life*.

I laughed, mostly because I thought it was wild that's how he thought I sounded. Being this close to someone mirrored how he saw me or even others.

"Let me go back to my room to get a jacket," I said as I grabbed my room key.

"Nah, you can use one of mine."

He grabbed the jacket from the closet and handed it to me as we were on the way out the door. My heart began to palpitate a bit faster than usual and my body tingled all over. This was the first time a guy ever offered me his jacket. I hope he couldn't hear the heartbeat that felt like it was pulsating through my entire being, even though I felt like it was connected to a speaker and could be heard throughout the building.

"Thanks," I said casually as if I wasn't documenting this entire moment in my head.

"No problem."

We made it out of the apartment and into the hall-way. He pressed the elevator button and it opened for us, which rarely happens. I pressed L to bring us to the lobby. I stood in the corner to the right and he took the corner to the left.

"Why are you staring at me?"

"I can't stare at a pretty girl wearing my jacket?"

"Oh my gosh," I said laughing, trying not to roll my eyes to my brain. My cheeks were now warm.

"Nevermind, I'll just stare at the floor then," he said tilting his neck down and glaring at the elevator floor.

"You're literally a clown."

The doors opened and he extended his arm outward, gesturing for me to walk out first. I enlarged my eyes as I was completely shocked, and he giggled.

There was no one in the lobby except for the building's security. It was a Tuesday evening so that's not that surprising.

"You two have a good evening," the security guard said while smiling at both of us, she's seen us together coming in or out several times. I feel like she likes seeing us together, like she's secretly rooting for us to make it.

In a way, I was too.

"Thanks," we said at the same time.

As he opened the door for me the wind welcomed us with a hello and we began to head east on 8th Street. He grabbed my hand, and we locked fingers. This was my second first of the evening, and I had to make sure I didn't freak out, he was now directly next to me.

Shoulder to shoulder he could probably hear everything going on within me. My heart and my thoughts raced. The guy who couldn't be in a relationship or be a good boyfriend was the same guy who grabbed his jacket for me, let me get off the elevator first, opened the door for me, and locked fingers with me to walk to the lake.

I had no clue what to make of any of it and even though I didn't know for sure, a piece of me didn't care. I was enjoying my night of firsts, at least I was trying to. My thoughts weren't flooding my brain to the point where I was removed from the present. I was there with his hand in mine.

I loved the city at night, I'd only been here for a few months and didn't think I could ever get over it.

"Why are you looking around so much?"

"I don't know," I lied.

"You know you could just tell me."

"I know you're from here so it's different, but I still can't believe I'm here in this city. I'm not used to it yet. I love it here."

"Yeah, being downtown always makes you feel like that. I still feel it sometimes."

"Really?"

"Yeah, it happens from time, especially when I have to do shoots for class. I'll find a random spot that I've never seen before or a place I passed a million times but noticed something different that time around and get inspired."

I looked at him while he spoke. He looked different to me when we weren't joking or being silly; he actually cared about something besides being a sleaze. *I wonder if anybody else saw him like this?*

"I don't think I ever asked you this, but what made you want to be a photographer?"

"To be honest, I don't know. It was kind of something I just tried and stuck with."

"Cool," I didn't really know how to respond.

After passing Wabash Avenue, we approached South Michigan Avenue. The streets were pretty quiet, which was typical for this time of day and we were about to cross the street. Grant Park looked ominous in the dark with the glare of the moonlight shining down; there were some skateboard kids out, joggers, and dog walkers. When I saw people just out and about in the city, I can't help but think about if they are taking in the city like I did, even wondering where all the cars that drove past were headed to.

The bright orange hand sign switched to the white walk man symbol, and we crossed together. Right then, being with Victor, I was happy I didn't date in high school. I didn't care about being walked to class in a poorly lit building with kids I couldn't wait to get away from. I was happy I took a chance to leave the only thing I knew to do something I wasn't really sure would work. I was sure I would've never found a boy I liked back home. I had pretty much met everyone I could've met within four years back in high school and that was all the convincing I needed that my guy was somewhere else. Now I had the chance to galavant in the streets with a boy I actually thought was interesting. I had no clue who he could be; he could be the next best photographer of our generation or own his own studio. I also had no clue what we could be. We, a term I'm typically not involved in because I'd never met someone who made me a *"we"* person or met a boy who included me in his plans, up until now I have been an *"I"* person with new blossoming thoughts that person could be changing. This first semester was full of firsts.

Trying to start my life over in a new city, forced me to take on new patterns, mostly new thoughts that I'd hoped I'd put into action. Whatever was old wasn't working for me, but I was used to them so I knew they would be hard to shake, I always commended myself for trying. Even though I just got here I was thinking long-term, some of it had to do with the city itself and the feeling it gave me. Some of it had to do with the opportunities that it had, with art galleries and museums spread throughout waiting for new curatorial talent. And some of it had to do with the guy who was holding my hand.

"What about you?"

"What?"

"What made you want to get into visual merchandising?"

"Oh, well visual arts are just a huge part of everything to me. Putting pieces together, designing a set-up and bringing visions to life, and then seeing people's reactions to it all ... I love it."

"So you just knew you loved it?"

"Yeah, it just clicked."

"Kind of like love at first sight?"

"I guess you could say that."

We passed Buckingham Fountain, crossed Lake Shore Drive, and finally made it to the lake.

My feet kind of hurt for a bit, still getting used to all the walking. Looking at it from this point of view it was nice because the lake looked like it went on forever with no end in sight.

I sat down on the concrete and Victor sat next to me.

I laid my head on his shoulder. My heart wasn't racing anymore but still, just like the waters we were staring at, time felt like it wasn't moving, in fact at this moment it felt like time didn't even exist. When he leaned in to kiss me on my forehead, I tried to keep my composure, but I melted.

A feeling I rarely felt, content. I didn't want a single thing to change or alter. This was it for me, I was here. Heart, body, and soul, all present.

I looked to the ground and smiled as that memory flooded back to me. So far, all my college memories were a mix of things I could never forget and something that I never thought I would experience. If I could put these memories on a DVD, I would watch them all the time and rewind them when I needed to be reminded of a lesson I had already learned, slap the same smile I had across my face now, or just laugh.

Going into this new year, I had some goals and wanted to leave some of the habits that got me nowhere last year behind. Pinpointing which ones could stay and which ones would have to get kicked to the curb. I know this might be a little hard since my Chicago habits were already formed, and I knew it was very easy to revert back to old behaviors. I didn't regret a single one of the choices I made because they all taught me something. I remembered I wanted my second semester to be different than my first. I chose to do these things because I hadn't done them before. I felt like I had to see what I was "missing out" on. I always wanted to make sure I was a well-experienced person and got everything I wanted out of life. I thought doing these things would help me do that, but as time went on and midterm week passed, I realized they weren't making me experienced in what I wanted to be experienced in. I was now a party girl, without any connections to anyone who had a career in the field I wanted. My school was too expensive for me to attend to not seriously strive to make something of myself. Every professor emphasized the power of networking more than any lesson they taught.

I had lost sight of all that because I feared missing out on something people had over-hyped; choosing to drink, go to parties, and dabble in drugs didn't instantly turn me into a young city sophisticate. This was such an alluring concept to me. I would blame it all on the TV shows I chose to watch. To be frank, I was upset that I even thought that it would; this was something I had to figure out on my own. But I recalled asking myself, *Will these activities make me a better artist?* I always thought artists were supposed to have an array of wild experiences to have something worth sharing with the world. Many of these experiences I now knew I did not want to partake in because one thing I did know is that everything isn't for everybody. I would even go a step further and say some things weren't meant for people to do. They just ended up tainting their lives with things that they believed would enhance their lives but made it worse. I couldn't think of one of my favorite rappers, singers, or painters who didn't participate in "extracurricular activities" and produce some masterpiece from it. Artists needed to create something that people could relate to, and I wanted to do the same thing. In the future, I could create an extremely elaborate museum exhibit that took lots of time and effort to put together. People could "*oooh* and *aaaah*" over it all they wanted to, but if someone didn't relate to it, it would've been for nothing.

I was sure I got this mentality after our visit to The Cube. Seeing real artists really out there and doing it inspired me the most.

"Do you think this outfit is cool?" I said doing a small spin in the living room. Black peplum tank top with sheer paneling on the cleavage, faux leather leggings, and black mid-calf riding boots with a silver buckle on the side was my outfit of choice for the evening.

"Yeah it'll work," Nicolette blandly stated.

"I know we're going over to Wicker, and I know this fit isn't necessarily hipster but it's the edgiest thing I could come up with."

"It's definitely not hipster, but for you I'd say it's as close as you're going to get."

"Touché."

"How long you got Savannah?" Nicolette yelled from the couch. She was always the first one ready between all of us. Laid out on the couch, scrolling through Twitter waiting for our glam sessions to be over.

"Give me like ten more minutes."

"So more like thirty?" I shouted from the bathroom, giggling trying not to mess up applying my berry-colored lipstick. MAC's "rebel" was my go-to when I felt like taking it up a few notches from my chapstick.

"Shut up!" she yelled back.

The apartment smelled like a mix of flat irons burning at 400F, Victoria's Secret Love Spell body spray, fresh cut limes, and New Amsterdam vodka. It was our unit's Saturday night scent.

"I just want to get there before it gets too packed. I actually want to meet Saba; I'd kill to be his stylist."

"So how does something like that actually work?" I plopped down in the armchair, finally done getting ready.

"So, The Cube is like a gallery space slash concert space. They usually have an exhibit that turns into a live performance."

"That's so lit, how'd you find out about this place?"

"My roommate last year took me, and it's been on my radar ever since," Nicolette said slowly, eyes still glued to her phone screen as she was scrolling.

"Cool."

"Sorry, I'm stalking Saba's tweets right now. I wonder if I could tell when he's going to get there."

"I love the fact that you're really going for this, it would be such a great opportunity."

"Girl I'm trying, you gotta make these moves or nothing major is ever going to happen."

I hadn't made many moves outside of class, besides sending some thank you notes to people I'd met at companies where we went on field trips. Maybe tonight could be my chance since it had an art gallery component.

"How do I look?" Savannah finally finished and sashayed to the living room.

"*Oooh*, I love the look. Especially that crop top," I said while giving her snaps for her ensemble.

A cream lace crop top, white bandeau underneath, black distressed skinnies, and all white Adidas shells.

"I totally thrifted it. I got it from Ragstock like two weeks ago."

"Ok let's get this pregame started," Nicolette finally stopped scrolling and sat up on the couch.

She filled three small shot glasses. One pink, one green, and one purple so we'd never forget whose drink was whose. All three glasses were full of cheap liquor that we were able to get the guy down the hall to get for us.

"Cheers to us and us doing the damn thing!" I had to let out this excitement, it being one of our last weekends on campus and me making it through all the times I got lost, the lonely time of not having friends, and being on my own for the first time of my life. I felt alive, and always wanted to feel that way.

A slight burning sensation went down my throat and my eyes were pinched shut. I hurried to grab a lime off the living room table.

"We have to do another one," Savannah insisted immediately after the first round.

"Ok, but I can't get too wasted. I'm also going there for business. Plus, we're taking the blue line there, so I want to be as alert as possible," Nicolette reminded us.

I would miss nights like this since I could only imagine how dull summer would be in comparison. On the brightside, there wouldn't be any more awkward public transportation rides that I didn't think I'd miss one bit.

"Ok, it's just one more," I smiled as the first shot was beginning to kick in. My body felt a bit looser, trying to keep my mind concentrated on where I was now, in my freshman year dorm with two girls that I spent most of my time with. Our living room walls once covered with concert tickets, posters of the Chicago "L" train routes, and random quotes we found on Pinterest were now barren as we approached our move out date.

Even though I was right here and now, my mind was already trying to make this a memory because I knew this moment would be over soon.

Pouring from the New Amsterdam bottle commenced, we went in for another clink. The second shot burned a little less than the first, no lime needed.

"O...M...G!" Nicolette shrieked.

"What?!" Savannah and I asked in unison.

"Saba just tweeted: 'OTW with a peace sign emoji!' We have to leave now!"

I felt like I almost broke my neck as I whipped my head around, scanning the room for my bag that was pre-packed with all of my essentials. I motioned away from the armchair, to my desk on the opposite side of the room. I was now officially ready for whatever the night had in store.

"Ok, I'm ready! Let's go!"

We were on the way out the door, swift movements, hearts racing. I felt a buzzing sensation from the top of my head to the very bottom of my feet. I knew we were going to have a good night, the second shot in my system also agreed.

"This elevator better hurry up!" Nicolette growled as she kept smashing the down button.

I was going to mention how that wasn't going to suddenly make the elevator appear, but I refrained.

Ding.

As the two doors separated, my eyes widened. There were so many people already there, but due to our time crunch I knew we were about to make this work. It was Saturday night; this was to be expected.

"Come on in! We can make room!" said some guy that I couldn't put a face to, the statement was coming from a short guy in the back. He was hidden behind the rest of the people on their way out to their designated excursions.

I sucked myself in like a Hoover and scooted on the elevator trying my best not to touch anyone even though we were packed like sardines. It was a mix of Axe body spray, mint gum, weed, and sweat swirling around this packed space.

I took a silent *whiff* as that combination of smells would bring back this moment when it was gone.

Ding.

The elevator stopped on floor nine.

"Hell no," I whispered with my head tilted toward the floor. Nothing got quite under my skin like when the elevator was packed, and it stopped on another floor. They would either come on and tighten the ride or use their common sense and just wait for another one to come. Honestly, Nicolette, Savannah, and I were the very last ones who could've made their way on this one. I was convinced one more body would have this thing reach max capacity. I hadn't gotten stuck on the elevator all year and I wasn't planning on it now.

The doors opened.

"Nah, I'm good," a girl waved her hand denying the entire elevator situation that was going down.

I was definitely relieved. My body slowly hunched forward; my right hand rapidly bounced against my thigh. A mix of the vodka, elevator fumes, and tight space made my head airy and desperately wanting to get off.

Finally at the lobby, I was the first one off the elevator. Appreciative for space in a way like I haven't felt before. Nicolette and Savannah trailed behind, and we were on our way.

"Are you a little nervous?" Savannah questioned Nicolette.

"Not really, I guess, the more I think about it the more I just want to get it over with," Nicolette stated calmly strutting out of the lobby into the night.

"Have you thought about what you're going to say?"

"Not really Savannah, I'm just going to introduce myself and let the rest flow."

"Nice."

I thought it was brave of Nicolette for sure. To know where one of the biggest upcoming rappers from the West side was going to be, get us on the list, and propose to style him definitely took guts. Unfortunately for Savannah, she pretty much knew she could probably never get us on the list anywhere or approach someone to legitimately style them.

"This is going to be so lit," I belted with my head toward the sky. Walking down State Street, making a left on Harrison, we were getting closer to the LaSalle Street blue line station.

"Of course, that's what Krista is ready for," Nicolette said through a chuckle.

This was true, but I also just wanted to lighten the mood Savannah was about to summon over us. I wanted nothing but good vibes on one of our last nights out before finals. We've all had our fair share of drama and disagreements. I didn't want tonight to be tainted with a speck of either.

The wind blew and hints of urine filled my nostrils as we made our way down the dusty steps of the LaSalle Street Station. I tapped my Ventra card on the scanner for entry and pushed my body through the metal rotating poles as the scanner screen turned green and read: "Go!" in white letters, pausing for a moment to wait for Nicolette and Savannah to make their way through. I slowly stepped backward to a wall to get out of the way of the other bustling commuters making their way down to the trains.

Once they made their way through, I followed behind them both. My body all of a sudden craved food as my mind reminded my stomach it hadn't had any food since breakfast.

"Is there going to be food at this thing?"

"I read somewhere that it's going to be light bites," Nicolette confirmed.

"Good, I'm starving."

On the train platform I lifted my head up to the screens that displayed the arrival times. The O'Hare bound train was arriving in four minutes. I grinned as I loved when there was barely a wait.

The tracks began to rattle as the train continued closer to our stop and its headlights brightened the tunnel along its path and came to a screeching halt. The cars were relatively empty, which made seat selection a breeze. I always tried to keep a distance between those who were already seated and sit next to my friends all at the same time. We took the row of seats that faced the windows with their backs facing the train station.

"Jackson is next."

"Do you know the theme of tonight's exhibit?" I turned my head to the left and asked Nicolette.

"No, I didn't really pay attention to that part," she responded while her right leg was tapping at nearly the same speed the train was going. I had never seen her like this, I was used to her being indifferent or just goofing off.

"You know if you're nervous it'll probably be best just to admit you are nervous before your foot taps a hole through the floor," I said while fighting back laughter.

Her face relaxed from its once tense, blank expression and I got a smirk out of her.

"You're right, it's just my first time putting myself out there and not just styling a student for a project or something. This would be serious," her foot slowed and rested on the train car's floor.

"True but try to think of it as not being too much different than working with a student. He's an up-and-coming artist, I'm sure he'll understand you trying to shoot your shot."

Nicolette's head nodded as she took my words in, her eyes looked upward as she was trying to recall all of her styling projects that led to this very moment.

"I still can't believe you're just going to go for it, he's not going to be expecting something like this," Savannah blatantly stated.

I squeezed the pole in front of me, completely blown away by this girl's statement. This went in the opposite direction of where I was trying to get Nicolette's headspace. I wanted her to feel at ease before she went in, be her normally bubbly self. She could do this with her eyes closed but Savannah's energy was not needed especially with us being a few stops away.

"Well Savannah, if I don't take a risk now I might never do it and be like some people who never show their work," Nicolette stated calmly yet sharp.

From there we all faced forward, gazing as the train swiftly passed posters pasted to the concrete walls of the tunnel until the train stopped at Division.

Girls glued in their mini dresses and bowler hats brushed past us on their way to Sushi Taku, some alternative pop music was blaring from The Perch Kitchen and Tap, and we already passed two guys with handlebar mustaches. All of Wicker Park was out tonight.

"Just a few more blocks, it's on Division & Leavitt Street," Nicolette announced as her pace quickened making her way slightly in front of Savannah and me.

I was also still positive I was hungry and would bee-line to the food table immediately upon entering the event.

In the distance, there was a white linoleum paneled garage with a line extending down the block. In three-dimensional, deep purple letters it read: "The Cube."

"Nicolette is that it?" I questioned while pointing directly ahead at it. I wasn't sure what I was expecting, but it definitely was not a garage.

"Yep, that's it."

The Cube was definitely a fitting name for the space then.

"I can't believe the line outside this place," Savannah added.

"Well, we don't have to worry about a line, that's the great part of being on the list," Nicolette stated still facing forward, eyes like lasers focusing on our destination ahead.

As we got closer to The Cube, my stomach growled. Its slight murmur made me look around to see if anyone else heard, but it appeared no one did. Besides being hungry, my body was signaling I was nervous. I wondered what connections I would make, if any at all. The last thing I wanted was to be attached at the hip to Savannah or just following Nicolette around like a lost puppy as she worked the room and actually tried to make something of herself. The thing was, I was still in the process of trying to figure out what I was trying to make myself to be. Nicolette had a niche market and a list of people she would potentially love to style. With my freshman year coming to an end, I'd be happy to just get my foot in the door at a gallery or volunteer at a museum or whatever was the first step to getting into this world.

I rolled my neck to the right to relieve the tension that my body was building as the thoughts rolled in, there was a cracking sound that filled the air.

"Damn Krista!" Nicolette shockingly responded to my louder than expected neck roll.

"Sorry, I guess I'm a little nervous too and didn't really feel it until now."

"Just remember the things you told me," Nicolette reminded me and winked.

She was right, I hated how I could give such great advice to others but had to remind myself of these same words repeatedly until they sunk in, even when I truly believed them in my spirit.

Eyes bugging, lip smacking, and people cursing underneath their breath, I'm sure I even heard someone say, "Who the hell do they think they are?" We were strutting to the front of the line, my head looking more to the ground as I was trying not to pay attention to every reaction that was happening around us.

"Nicolette plus two," Nicolette said as we were finally directly in front of the gatekeeper himself.

His bald head bent down to review his clipboard that was tightly grasped, held close and upward to not reveal a single name that was printed on this highly regarded list. There was silence for a moment, I noticed his pupils travel and get closer to the bottom of the page. The crisp paper made a smacking noise as he flipped to the other sheet. My fingers started to tap against my thigh. I don't believe Nicolette would've dropped the ball on this, she was too determined about the whole plan, and it was the only thing I could recall her gushing about for the last few weeks. It was just awkward standing in front of him as if we were waiting for some big reveal to take place.

"*Ahh* ... Nicolette plus two, I finally found you," he said grabbing a neon yellow highlighter from his back pocket and marking a straight line across the paper. He stepped aside to make room for us to enter.

"Thanks!" Nicolette exclaimed and walked right in.

My fingers stopped tap dancing on my thighs as I was relieved that there wasn't a mix up and we could just go in.

"Enjoy your night ladies."

Dark room, cobalt light bouncing off the walls and reflecting on the crowd, and soft R&B ballads serenaded the space.

"I'm in love with this place," my voice raised a bit to ensure Nicolette and Savannah heard me.

"Yeah, it's really cool!" Savannah echoed.

Nicolette nodded as her eyes scanned every crevice of the room. Her complete concentration was on locating Saba and delivering a killer pitch.

"Don't forget to have a little fun while you're here, look where we are," I was fully aware of her mission, and I was also fully aware of the fact we were in a gallery space with good music, some influential people present, and great vibes.

"I won't forget but I feel like if I don't hurry up and get this out of the way, I'm going to explode," Nicolette explained, eyes still darting.

"First, don't think about this as something you want to just get out of the way, you're always going to remember this night as making a real move in your career. Second, let's just grab a drink and some food. It could help you relax a bit."

"You're right, I am going to remember this night. But I just spotted him, and I don't think I could have some fun until this gets done," Nicolette declared sternly.

"Ok, you've got this! I'm going to grab something to eat before my stomach caves in."

"Good luck!" Savannah reassured.

"Thanks guys, I'm going in."

And just like that Nicolette detached herself from our Three Musketeer huddle and squeezed through the mass group of people chatting and holding drinks. I watched her for a while like a proud parent sending a child off to school for the very first time hoping for the best outcome.

Little crackers with slices of cheese, rolled sandwiches, wings, and assorted fruit trays filled the long buffet table. I hoped my eyes gave my stomach the memo to relax, as it was finally getting what it craved. I snatched a miniature plastic plate and filled it up with the small rolled sandwiches and stood by the table for a little while. Popping one in my mouth, my eyes closed for a moment as I savored the quick bite. I could not network on an empty stomach, so I convinced myself I'd coast here until I was ready to immerse myself with everyone else. I also needed another drink or two so I could loosen up a bit.

"I circled the room, but I felt stupid because I really didn't know what to do," Savannah admitted as she walked towards me and the table full of refreshments.

I put my hand over my mouth as I chewed, I wasn't that surprised by her statement, and I didn't really know what to say.

"You didn't find a group you could just finesse your way into or a person hanging solo you could talk to?" I managed to get out as I was finishing up one of my sandwiches.

"I kind of started to make my way over to people a few times but I just couldn't so I just looked at some of the pieces."

I wasn't judging as I was practically in a corner stuffing my face instead of socializing in a setting this was designated for.

"What makes you the most nervous about talking to them?" I asked hoping her response would help me figure out what to say next. In these instances, I believed you either had the ability to just put yourself out there or you didn't. I couldn't say that to her though, I didn't want to hurt her feelings.

"Honestly just going up to a group is way too scary for me, and what do I say when I walk up to a person? It just feels weird to me."

Lips pursed and switching them from side to side, my brain contemplated the best words to say. It wasn't the easiest thing in the world to just walk up and start talking to people you didn't know. The thing was it took just a smidge of confidence and Savannah was lacking in that department. I also didn't think I was the best person to give a crash course on the topic.

"You're right, a group can definitely be intimidating." I assured, my eyes squinted to search the room for any singles who didn't give off the vibe that they were too intellectual to have a regular conversation.

Savannah had her head down and was fidgeting with her nails. This was not how this night was going to go for us.

"Even though you're scared there's plenty of people just standing in front of the art. You could just act like you're admiring it too and come up with something to say."

"That could worrrkkk ..." Savannah stretched out the end of work until it sounded like a two-syllable word.

"Girl you gotta make it work, we didn't come out tonight for nothing," I stated to Savannah and myself as I threw my mini plate away along with my last finger sandwich. My stomach was good for now, and we did not get all dressed up to stand in a corner and clean our nails or stuff our faces with catered food.

"Ok, you're right. I just gotta have a drink first, those shots have worn off for me and I'm going to need a bit more liquid courage."

"That's cool with me, but after that no more stalling."

808s boomed, the floor underneath me vibrated, I could feel the beat in my chest as I grabbed Savannah's hand as we maneuvered through a sea of people. As we were excusing ourselves and getting by, I momentarily got a glance of Nicolette. Her smile glistened as she talked, her hands were in the air which was a good sign because she spoke with her hands anytime she got really excited.

"Two vodka tonics," Savannah requested as she leaned over the bar.

"Coming right up."

"Can you make them strong? More vodka than tonic," I added as I was looking for a bit more of a buzz and I'm pretty sure Savannah wouldn't mind.

"Sure thing sweetie."

Drinks in hand I swayed from side to side to the beat and shook off any jitters that were lingering within me. Savannah was stiffly sipping and bobbing her head.

"You can at least throw in a little two step," I joked.

"I could, but there's a guy staring directly at you and has been since we've got over here."

My sway slowed down until it completely halted.

"Are you sure?" I questioned, turning my head trying to identify who it could be.

"Don't look!" Savannah yelped and shook her hand feverishly.

I clearly broke an obvious rule. I felt stupid for turning and actually looking for the guy Savannah said had his eyes on me.

"Ok don't act weird but he's coming over here now," Savannah managed to get out through gritted teeth.

"Really?" I asked, straightening my back, and finishing off my drink in one gulp. So much for our prep before we approached people to talk to.

"Yes, just act natural. He's really cute."

I deeply inhaled, and slowly exhaled, "Ok."

Savannah raised her eyebrows and grinned.

"How are you ladies doing?" I heard a voice say right behind me.

I swiveled and my eyes brightened, my face was warm from the vodka. I hoped he couldn't tell I was blushing. Savannah was right, he was cute. Arguably the cutest guy that had ever approached me.

"We're having a pretty good time," I said looking right into his piercing hazel eyes.

"I'm glad to hear that, a lot of work goes into planning these things and you never really know how they're going to turn out."

"Cool, so you work here?" Savannah asked, still sipping on her last drops of her vodka tonic.

"Actually, I own the place."

Savannah coughed several times after that bomb dropped. My brain was still stuck repeating the words, "I own the place." We were hesitant about starting conversations with people who were just standing around admiring art, and now we're trying to keep our composure while we talk to the owner of the gallery.

"There's actually a piece over there that I haven't gotten a chance to look at closely," Savannah stated as she slowly walked away from us both.

"Are you sure?" I questioned her while my eyes widened slightly. I couldn't believe she was actually going to leave me alone with this guy that we just met. I was nervous, my brain was already spinning with conversation prompts. What does a college freshman talk to a gallery owner about?

"Yeah, I'm sure, talking to you gave me an idea. You should also take some of your own advice," Savannah winked and dashed away.

She gave me no time for a rebuttal; she was also right. Some of those words I freely gave had the perfect opportunity to be put to use at this very second.

"So what advice did you give your friend?" he leaned closer and asked with his voice raised.

"I was just telling her how she should just go for things, and stop being the one holding herself back," I was relieved he was the one that got the ball rolling for our conversation.

"What do you think you need to stop holding yourself back?"

I couldn't tell if I was tipsy or if his eyes were naturally glistening. I also was enchanted by the cobalt light reflecting off his caramel skin. My conversation prompts and wit were slowly escaping my brain, my fingertips began drumming on the outside of my thigh as I started to draft up the right thing to say. I wanted it to be honest, yet vague. I just met the guy.

"I'm not really sure anymore, this has been the most indescribable year of my life."

"Really? How so?" his brows furrowed and lips turned with a smidge of a grin. He seemed like he talked to women and made their night for a living.

"To sum it all up, I'd say it's just college and figuring it all out," I wasn't completely satisfied with my response, but it was already out. I didn't think it was enough time in the night to discuss the drama with trying to find an apartment, navigating a new city, feeling things for your man who isn't your man, and doing my best to focus on the main reason I came here, which was becoming who I was really meant to be.

"Don't worry too much, we're all just trying to figure it out but it's good you're in school. What do you go to school for?"

"Visual Merchandising, but I want to do curatorial work at a gallery or museum."

"That's what's up, you're in the right place."

I grinned, hearing those words felt reassuring. Id often felt like I wasn't in the right place, or trying to create one all on my own because that was the only time I felt like I fit anywhere. Running around this city, seeking experiences that I had never felt before, breaking the mold of my high school past, and doing anything that made me feel alive was what gave me the time to mold that space.

"Thanks, that means a lot."

"You're welcome, but next year if you need an internship or just want to get your foot in the door and help out from time-to-time, you definitely can stop by here."

My inner being was trying to stop my outer self from showing too much excitement. I know I'm a freshman but that doesn't mean I want to come off like an absolute rookie. I blinked to refrain my eyes from growing twice their size. My body loosened; I was standing stiff as a board the entire conversation. This was my door opening, one of those lightbulb moments. Not necessarily a firework moment as this wasn't my "big break" but I knew this was a step in the right direction.

"Really? That would be amazing!" I only questioned because a part of me couldn't believe this was happening.

"Yeah, you gotta start somewhere," he said while tilting his body to the right and fiddling around in his camouflage cargo pocket.

"I'd love to!"

"Here's my card, reach out when you're back next fall."

"I will."

"Alright, I look forward to hearing from you but before I go, I just realized I never got your name."

"Krista ... Krista Clark."

"It was nice to meet you, Krista," he said as he began to make his way through the crowd and get back to working the room.

"Nice to meet you too," I said, still floating from my moment. I looked around the gallery as if someone had a hidden camera ready to let me know the jig was up and all of that was just a joke. I took a deep breath, slowly in and slower out. I made the mental note to believe that good things are real and not only were they real but that they could happen to me.

I made my way through the gyrating bodies holding drinks and loud chit chat. I saw Nicolette and Savannah on the other side of the room, my body buzzing from excitement and alcohol. I couldn't wait to share what just happened and get the rundown of how things went with Nicolette and Saba.

"Soooo... how did everything go?" I expressed my wonder immediately upon arrival.

"Girl I was so nervous at first, but he was cool, which I was expecting, but I didn't want to come off like I knew him because that's definitely a groupie move," Nicolette was talking fast which was another key indicator she was excited.

"Tell her the good part already!" Savannah squealed.

"Okay, okay so he agreed to a trial styling session. So, it'll give us the opportunity to see if we mesh, and if I'm a good fit for his team. He only likes to work with people he actually likes, it's not just about the clothes."

"That's amazing!" I was genuinely happy for her, things looked like they were just starting for us.

"I know, excited isn't even the word to describe how I'm feeling right now. I'm on a high, my hands are still shaking," Nicolette held out her vibrating hand for solid proof.

"But tell us how things went with gallery guy," Savannah asked, raising her eyebrows, oozing intrigue.

"What's with the funny brows? Who's gallery guy?" Nicolette questioned needing to be fully looped in.

"The guy who owns this gallery could not stop staring at Krista while we were at the bar. I'm telling you his eyes were glueddd."

"Well, it was more to it than that, he didn't say anything majorly flirty or ask me out. We just talked about school, life, and he told me to hit him up when I'm back in the city if I wanted to help around the gallery."

The last thing I wanted was my moment to be tainted with insinuating he was hitting on me and that was his sole intention. The talk was mildly flirtatious yet professional, I could admit it fell somewhere in the in-between.

"Wow, that's good that just happened for you." Nicolette stated plainly.

"It was a shock for me for sure, I wasn't expecting that to happen tonight." I felt like I was defending the situation instead of celebrating it.

"He was cute though; eye candy and art are definitely the ideal work environment."

"What got into you?!" I asked surprised that this much enthusiasm was coming from Savannah.

"Maybe it was the drinks, your words, the good news ... I don't know but I'm happy for my friends."

I glanced over to Nicolette, waiting for something. Something that didn't bring the moment down, reciprocating at least an ounce of support that I did for her.

"It is good news. I just want you to be careful with a guy like that. It's just out of the blue to me."

She never met the guy, didn't see him, didn't utter a word to him so I didn't really know what to make of her warning.

"Sure, I'll keep my eye out for anything sus."

Even though I was going to miss the city and feared being bored out of my mind at home, this moment reminded me it was going to be nice to have a break from both Nicolette and Savannah. Between the need of constantly having to babysit Savannah's feelings and making sure the spotlight was on Nicolette 24/7, I was the living definition of the word exhausted.

This was the type of news I had wished I was sharing with Valentina. Right now, she'd actually be thoroughly excited for me and leave the knock-off motherly advice for the woman who actually birthed me. This trio dynamic had a tendency to feel like a bike with training wheels, not all the time but often enough. The Cube now looked smaller than before as my brain felt like it was shaking from irritation, and I was ready to make an exit.

I stared down at the crisp, cream, matte business card. Smooth center, sharp edges, and the name Tony Malik shining in forest green lettering. I giggled because I just noticed I never knew what his name was until now and the negativity from Nicolette didn't matter. I wasn't going to let her suspicion ruin the moment I just had, it was mine and it didn't matter if I got celebrated by her. No one could take that away from me, this moment was mine.

Even before college, I felt like God created me to add to people's lives on earth, not just to take. I wanted to do that through my craft, I just wasn't sure how. I wanted to create something people could feel and be happy that they showed up to view. I would get joy from just knowing I was a part of putting it together. I didn't want just fame and admiration without the ability to inspire others and create art people could resonate with. I had to now figure out how to do that the way He would have me to.

Stepping out of my comfort zone and going out more, or just going out period was me looking for something I didn't have and getting a break from my routine of class, getting food, checking out a tourist site, and watching TV. The beginning was rough, and I didn't really know who to express my concerns to. Peers were a definite no as everyone looked like they knew where they were going and had the map to where X marked the spot. So I turned to someone I could trust to not really tell anyone anything.

"You can't be the only one that is or looks lost," Kathryn tried her best to console me as best she could over the phone.

I was resting my head on the corner of the back cushion of the armchair in the living room of my dorm that still felt foreign to me. Curled up, but I felt like crumbling and relieved that no one else was in the apartment. I couldn't decompress around people I barely knew.

"Well, if I'm not, everyone else is really good at hiding it."

"Exactly, they could just be hiding it. There's no way everyone just got there and knows everything."

"Well, some of the students are from here, and I did miss some of the freshman meet up events because I was spending time with you guys."

"Overall, this is what you really wanted, you just got there so just give it time."

Her words were true. I wanted to be here, I chose this place and before the first few weeks of living the experience instead of fiddling with a fantasy I thought it was what I truly wanted. It just didn't feel like what I expected it would.

"I'm just telling you how I feel, dad would combust if I wanted to leave after he let me come."

"I could hear him losing his mind now if he even caught wind of you wanting to come home."

He was the least of my concerns as my headache was brewing from the storm of thoughts that raged on inside of me. *Should I stay? How much time is enough time to know something isn't right for you? Where would I go if I didn't stick it out here? I read somewhere college was free in Europe, I could roll the dice there?*

"Hellooo?" Kathryn questioned with a sprinkle of worry in her tone.

"I'm sorry, I just blanked out there for a second." I shook my own head in hopes that would get me out of it and straightened my body to where my back rested upright in the seat.

"It's cool, things are kind of weird without you here." Kathryn replied as her voice lowered.

I could feel her sadness through the phone. I never thought about how me leaving would have affected everyone. I wasn't really sure what to say.

"Really?"

"Yeah, mom cried for like a week straight and dad has just been working nonstop. I don't have anyone to really talk to."

"We should set up a schedule for FaceTime or something," I suggested hoping that would lift her spirits.

I was finally getting used to my class schedule and I still hadn't found a job, adjusting to the new scenery and people was my new full-time gig.

"That would be cool."

"We could even create a countdown to Thanksgiving since it'll be the first time I'll be back home since I left." I hoped this would feel like some sort of consolation prize for my current physical absence.

"Yessss!" Kathryn shrieked.

I hoped by then I'd have some kind of routine or find my groove, a friend, something ...

Second guessing myself was now my first instinct. I decided to ride this wave out to shore, I believed the tide was sure to change. Something had to come up, at least that was what I told myself every morning on my way to class while weaving through the masses of students trying to make their mark just like me.

"Don't tell mom or dad but I was thinking I made a mistake in coming here." Those thoughts were swirling after completing my second week.

"Don't be dramatic Krista, you've only been there a few weeks."

"I'm not being dramatic. I'm just telling you how I feel. I spend all my time alone here. It feels like an extended vacation or something."

"Well, what are you going to do?"

I could have left if I didn't care about what others thought. But also, what would I think of myself if I just gave up? My brain would hunt for the rest of my life with "What ifs..."

"I don't know."

"I believe you'll figure it out," Kathryn said in a dry but sincere manner.

That's just how she was, and it was typically what I needed when I was having one of my emotional crises.

During that time, I felt like one of those days I would pick the right night to go out, or I'd pick the right party and my life could change for the better, forever. Most of the time that was just me letting the beauty of the city talk to me, it was cliché I know, but I still thought it. I was not naive enough to think that anymore; I'm not completely jaded after my freshman year, I just knew better now. At least I thought so, sitting there it was easy to say until my dad's truck was headed west on I-94 and I saw the skyline. I'd hear whispers that tantalized my need for adventure and was convinced otherwise. Now, if things weren't pushing me in the right direction toward my career or anything positive, I didn't want anything to do with it. All that stuff got old after a while anyway. After midterms, our grades made Nicolette, Savannah, and me not even want to hear the word party.

I ended up with all Bs and one A that I had to do extra credit to get. All I had to do was go to an art gallery opening on a Saturday morning and listen to the "artist to watch" speak and write a three-page synopsis, but still, I felt it was cutting into my sleep on a Saturday. The sleep I deprived myself of at the beginning of the semester was now trying desperately to catch up. My body was still recovering and telling me I was not cut out for the constant party life, maybe just in doses but not a weekly tradition. Seeing all those Bs that very well could've been As motivated me to do better next year because I was capable of better. I know a B wasn't failing, but I'd always been a nerd and getting all As was something I made a goal.

I also knew that wasn't the only thing that needed to change next year.

During the school year, I continually debated what I wanted from Victor. He left me feeling confused since the connection was there without question. He made me feel like no boy ever had, and a piece of me feared that another boy could never do the same. The problem wasn't the connection but was the commitment, and I hated that more than anything. This specific emotion always made me feel like my mind was tossing and turning, and it made me anxious. Sometimes he wouldn't text me or come to my room and visit for days or weeks. I wouldn't text him either in fear I would look clingy or desperate, I figured if he wanted to see me, he would.

Ever since I met him, I thought about him all the time, like if I thought something was funny I wanted to share it with him or tell him all about my day which most people did when they had a boyfriend. But I told myself I didn't want a boyfriend because he would be a distraction. This didn't make me not want a boyfriend though. I learned to enjoy my alone time after a while and didn't have to answer to anyone. Most people I knew who were in a relationship with their boyfriends acted like they were their dads. They would tell them what to do and hound them through constant calls and texts. I wasn't down for that, and I didn't want to be responsible for someone else's emotional baggage, I already had enough of my own. The part that killed me the most was that I had invested a lot of my emotions into someone, and didn't know what I wanted from him exactly. I always asked myself whether I wanted him to be my friend or boyfriend and no clear answer came from this question. All I knew was that I enjoyed his company more than anyone else's there; he made me laugh, we could talk for hours, and whenever we hung out he would always say something I wouldn't expect him to say. Most of the unexpected things he said were jokes about us having sex. I would always roll my eyes and act like what he said was so far-fetched, but I was 100% enticed.

Even though he was a funny guy, and I felt like we got along he was very flaky. Whenever he brought up doing something with me, we would never do it, or it would get rescheduled, or modified to some capacity. His mood could change in an instant and he could go from being a nice guy to an asshole in a flash.

"How was your day?" he asked.

"It was okay, I guess. Class was just class. This one girl literally tried to one up me during presentations, but I guarantee the teacher liked mine better. Oh, and I tried this one French restaurant for lunch today; it was delicious. I think you and I should..." I looked up and he appeared to be less than interested and fully immersed into the TV.

He stopped listening.

"Victor!" I yelled and threw a pillow at him.

"What?"

"Why aren't you listening to me?"

"You just kept going on and on, I stopped listening after you said something about class."

I looked at him with my brows furrowed. He was an asshole, but he took the time to be honest, which I didn't know if I hated or appreciated; he puzzled me. *Would this be us two years down the line after I decided to give him a chance and realized I was in a long-term relationship with this guy who was more into his Netflix queue than me?* With no clear answer in sight, I made up that it was worth figuring out who he was.

He was also the type of guy that said what came into his mind all the time. He did things with little to no thought. He was completely opposite of me, and I was intrigued by that. For instance, he was not the type of person to be sitting on a bench, on a bridge, above a riverbank thinking about freshman year of college and about how he could make next year better. The thing I hated most about Victor was the fact he got around a lot, in fact that was the only thing that kept me from giving into him completely. I probably couldn't count how many people he has had sex with on all my fingers and toes; it was just too much. The rumors ate away at my brain and that would be the end of us; that bothered and scared me all at the same time. I knew I didn't want someone like that as my first boyfriend and be the first person I ever had sex with. When he was through with these girls he left with no remorse. *Why would he treat me any differently?*

Even though I had all these facts, I felt like I couldn't make up my mind about what I was going to do. So, I decided to pray about it. I couldn't keep bringing it up to Nicolette or Savannah. I was more than tired of talking to them about the whole thing.

"So do you like him or not?" Nicolette asked me as she poured some cheap peach Moscato into three mugs.

"I'm not 100% sure yet, I'm still trying to figure it out," I said as I was mixing the cupcake batter. The kitchen smelled sweet, and I wished things in my life felt the same.

"Well, you better hurry up and figure it out. I saw him and Bria hanging out yesterday on the way back from class," Savannah added from the living room as she decided what movie we would watch.

"Are you serious? What were they doing?" I stopped stirring the confetti cake goodness because this was breaking news.

"Yes, and you know that's his ex, so..."

I didn't need to be reminded of the fact she was his ex, I was very aware of that annoying fact.

"What if they got back together?" Nicolette asked as she left the kitchen on her way to the living room.

I'd die.

"Don't say that," I said because I honestly couldn't bear that idea. He told me several times that they got together before classes even started and they only got together because they hooked up and he thought she was kind of cool.

"Do you think they still hook up?" Savannah asked.

"Do you guys want cupcakes or not?" I asked completely ready to throw the batter in the trash if they continued talking about this subject that was making my insides turn in knots.

"Krista calm down, it's not that serious."

"It's not that serious because you guys don't feel like you lo…"

"We don't feel like we what?" Nicolette asked me, egging me on to finish.

I wouldn't dare.

"Yeah Krista, what?"

"Nothing, just forget I said anything."

I wasn't sure if I loved him or not and I didn't want a word to come out of my mouth if I wasn't sure.

"All I know is if you feel like you love anyone, you better do something about it. Because I can't take more months of this yo-yo behavior."

I couldn't either.

People tend to care about other people's problems for so long before they get uninterested. Unlike people, God never gets tired of hearing from you, even if it's the same problem over and over. So I knew if I wanted to talk to Him all day long about anything at all, I could.

The night I remembered the most between us was two weeks after winter break resumed. It was February, ice and slush on the roads, and temperatures were borderline unbearable. During that break, I thought about him more than ever and at the time was thinking about us getting together. It was the beginning of February, and we were bored that night in his room, so I suggested we play 21 questions.

"You can ask me 21 questions and I have to tell the truth; then you do the same," I said explaining the rules. I knew this was going to be interesting.

His eyes widened, eyebrows raised, and he sported an ear-to-ear grin as if this was the best idea he'd ever heard.

He asked his questions first.

"If you had a superpower, what would it be?"

"Easy. I would be able to fly."

"What's your favorite season?"

"Summer, because that's when my birthday is."

"Are you a virgin?"

"Yes." This was something I didn't have an explanation for; the opportunity never presented itself to me. It was a secret that I worked overtime to stay that way.

It was quiet for a moment. I was ready for him to fire out another question but by the look on his face I could tell he didn't believe me. I also felt my palms getting sweaty, that was something I didn't want him, of all people, to know about me. He probably would make endless jokes or tell others, and I wouldn't be able to live it down. He would not want to have sex with me because I had no experience.

"You know you said we have to tell the truth," he said completely suspicious of the answer I gave to the last question.

"I know," I said assuring him that I didn't forget the rules of the game I suggested we play.

"Have you ever thought about me sexually?"

I took a gulp, I had never said things like this out loud, but I had to tell the truth.

"Yes," I said quickly as if that would have made the answer mean something different. I wished I had the superpower of being able to control every thought that entered my mind. Yes, I'm attracted to Victor. Yes, we were friends. No, I did't want to have sex with someone who had sex with everyone, and no I did't know why it was taking me forever to make up my mind. I didn't want to regret not exploring the person because of the persona. I didn't want to think about him that way, because every time I did, I felt bad, like the thought didn't belong in my brain. I didn't think it aligned with who I was as a person; we were so different. But from time to time it crept in.

I felt myself blush and my body temperature began to rise.

Victor grinned and looked satisfied, it seemed he found enjoyment in making me nervous, mixed in with the fact he now knew he was the star of my daydreams *and* nighttime fantasies.

He asked me the rest of my questions and then it was my turn.

I wanted to ask him if he ever thought of me sexually, but that would be me wasting 1 of my 21 questions that I already knew the answer to.

"Do you want to live in Chicago forever?"

"No, I'll probably go to California or Texas because of the weather."

"What's your favorite food?"

"Pizza, I can eat it at any time of day."

"Where do you want to go with your career?"

"I love shooting nature shots, so I would work for any place that does that."

I asked him questions about his family, what he was like when he was in high school, things about his past, and what he wanted to be like in his future.

I had one question left. I couldn't help it; I made it about me. I wanted to know what his intentions were with me. I felt it would let me know how he saw me.

"What do you want from me?" As the words left my mouth, I noticed I sounded demanding but uncertain because I was afraid of the answer. It was my best attempt at asking "What are we?" without being *super* obvious about it.

"Friendship and sex," he said just as casually as his former answers.

I was shocked, but I refused to let it show on my face. I wanted to appear just as cool and nonchalant as he did, but I was imploding. I was internally freaking out about his answer because I was a virgin, and he was the furthest from it. Or was it because I wasted my winter break thinking about someone who never wanted me to be his girlfriend. It also could've been because I was trying to love someone who wasn't that lovable.

All I knew was that I wanted the truth and I got it. He didn't want a girlfriend, just a friend with benefits. I never understood why people wanted that, especially why *he* wanted that with *me*. We were too special, a feeling that you didn't get twice. These things added more confusion to an already mixed situation, and I could not afford to add any more confusion to this predicament. This would never work out; it could go on like that forever. One wanted to call it quits and then there would be no more friendship. However, I only knew this from the observation of others.

This game made me wish I had asked that question sooner, way before I put a couple of months and many thoughts into the feelings he didn't have for me. I wanted to ask him if he could only have one, friendship or sex, which would he choose, but the game was over. I was too scared, and fear of rejection glued my mouth shut. My brain repeatedly screamed, "You've got to be kidding me!" Even though I wasn't deadset on being his girlfriend, I felt like I was led on and had been deceived by him. I could even say I had deceived myself by trying to get something from a person who didn't have what I was looking for. It was like going to Taco Bell and asking for a double cheeseburger, it just didn't make sense! But the truth always had a way of defeating deception.

This game made me realize how Victor didn't know me at all. He had never really taken the time to because he only had one thing on his mind, while he made time to spend with an abundance of other females. I was never a priority, and neither were the boatload of other girls he spent time with.

After that, I remember I took a break from seeing him. I didn't want to, but my mind convinced me it had to be done. I was no longer anticipating a knock on my door from him, eating with him in the cafeteria, or cuddling while watching movies with him in his room. I needed time to regroup and get out of the whirlwind of emotional chaos that we both created.

It was hard to stay away from him. I found myself taking the stairs more often to avoid an unwanted run in, switching the time I ate at the food hall, and whipping my head around to watch my back anytime I was out and about on campus. Although this was the case, I missed him being around. He was the first friend I made at my school. I never told him, but he meant a lot to me. My brain knew, and my heart felt that I couldn't have given him a chance to be with me, or *not* with me in his case. It wasn't the right time for us, and I felt it never would be; unless Victor changed ... *could Victor change?* This was the question that kept me up late at night on my stiff twin-sized dorm mattress. I needed my heart's feelings to catch up to the truths stored in my brain. Even after I knew the truth and got my feelings hurt, a small part of me wanted him to be my first *and* my boyfriend.

Two whole months had passed, and we ended up running into each other on the elevator; even with my best efforts it was only a matter of time before this happened. I tried not to act awkward, but the air between us felt very thick and I could tell we both were feeling nervous. I wanted to pretend like I just saw him yesterday and we hadn't gone a long time without seeing each other.

I wanted to ask him how he had been doing and if he missed me, but my mouth wouldn't open. The sting of rejection lingered.

"Hey," was the only thing he said like these past weeks with the lack of my presence hadn't affected him at all.

"Hey," I said flatly, matching his tone exactly.

I pressed the button for the seventeenth floor. Victor pressed the button for the sixteenth floor.

It was quiet for a while, so I just stared at the lit-up seventeenth floor button as if that would make time go by faster. *God please let this time fly.*

When the door to his floor opened, I was relieved, and sad. I always pictured us seeing each other again much differently than this. I thought he would at least be kind of happy to see me and want to know how I had been.

"So, are you coming or what?" he asked as he got off on his floor.

My heart jumped. I was more than surprised. I leaned forward to make my way off, yet my right leg felt planted to the floor. I hesitated for a moment, but I got off with him. I thought we were never going to talk to each other again after our game of 21 questions. I didn't want that to be the case, so I got off the elevator. Walking into his room felt odd but with a heavy sense of familiarity. Even though time had passed it looked the same as it did two months ago, nothing changed.

His bed was unmade, laundry was piled up in a corner of his room. His table and TV were surrounded by game systems and video games. His drawers were open and revealed his junk and empty condom box. His blinds were open with a killer view of The Willis Tower. I remembered coming into his room for the first time and telling him how much I loved the view. Everything about the room still screamed typical Victor. Yet, it all felt unfamiliar because of how long it had been since I'd been in there.

"So, I heard your new life motto was get money and have sex without emotion."

I honestly couldn't believe I said that. It was something that I had to let flow because it bothered me. I thought I might as well address one of the many elephants in the room.

"What? How'd you hear that?" he scoffed.

"Let's just say through a mutual friend," I said trying to have a sense of mystery about me, but really Nicolette heard him say it to someone on the elevator and she told me. I wondered what events went down in my absence that made him want to publicly brand himself with that slogan. *Thank God, Nicolette and Victor didn't know each other, it was clutch to have an unexpected source deliver a message.*

"I heard you hooked up with some dude at a party," he mimicked my faux nonchalant-ness.

"No, you didn't."

"Yeah, I did. One of my friends said they saw you, but I said that didn't sound like the Krista I remember," he stated while grinning.

The Joker had nothing on him.

"Well, I could be different," I said trying to add some mystique and allure that I wished existed naturally.

"You could be, but I want to let you know I like you a lot. Like a *lot*, I just can't be in a relationship right now."

That sentence was only half of what I wanted to hear. I was relieved that I wasn't the only one who felt that way.

"So, when will you be ready?"

"I don't know," Victor sighed heavily.

I decided not to go on any further with the questions I had for him. I was enjoying our time together, and I felt like it would've ruined everything. Discussing a relationship that we may or may not be in one day was tiring and something I didn't have the emotional energy for.

Looking back, that was dumb, I never held him accountable for his actions, that gave him permission to carry on the way he did. I gave the excuse that I'm not his girlfriend so I can't tell him what to do, but even though that was the case, he was my friend. Friends look out for each other, no matter how weird the friendship may be.

I took a deep breath and exhaled, anxiety was being lifted from me and my brain was decluttering. My freshman year was a rollercoaster to say the least. I learned I hated the weird, murky, in-between gray area that life's situations had put me in. The black and white was clear because I knew where I stood in a situation and more importantly relationships.

I didn't know this at first, but having time away gave me time to reflect. I thought I knew him, but now looking back I realized he never told me anything about him that truly mattered. I always felt the need to have to play some sort of game to get anything out of him.

I believe relationships are the most important aspect of human existence. If they weren't, I wouldn't be sitting on a bench, on a bridge, over a riverbank reflecting on a relationship that caused me to be in the biggest gray area I've ever been in my entire life.

I learned that everyone had a role to play in my life. Trying to make people something they are not and forcing them to play a role they were not meant to play leads to pain.

I have seen now, after all these months, Victor wasn't meant to be my boyfriend. Just because I met him at a time when I was alone and I liked having him around didn't mean I had to try to make more of it, especially when we never gave each other clear signals.

"He was meant to be my friend, and that's precisely what I needed at the time we met," I said out loud trying so hard to convince all parts of myself of this.

I now knew that when I'm ready to be in a relationship I won't focus on some magical, all-consuming feeling but to focus on the reality that is presented to me. To love the real person who I am with and not what I would ideally like them to be. I'd state what I want from the beginning and would ask them in a direct manner instead of playing a game, and not pretend we were going somewhere when we were both actually on a carousel of confusion.

I learned to do better next time. This year was a second shot, I no longer felt anxious about it. I didn't see it then, but everything happened the way it was supposed to.

"God if I'm not supposed to be with him, then whom? I'd love for you to just make it obvious," I groaned aloud.

prepping

"You're supposed to be here helping me decide what should come back with me, not trying to keep clothes for yourself," I fussed as Kathryn was sliding hangers one by one and examining which one of my pieces was hers for the taking.

"If you think about it, donating clothes is the perfect way to get rid of things you don't want," Kathryn joked.

"The operative words of what you just said are things you don't want. I have to approve of everything you're thinking about taking before you try to scurry away with it."

"You got it boss," she said as she saluted me like a sergeant.

"You are so irritating," I barely got the words out while laughing.

I stood in front of my wardrobe trying to decide what was good enough to come back to school with me. A piece of me couldn't believe it was that time again, and the other was just excited to escape the basement. I knew a lot of people hated packing, but I always enjoyed it. This time I loved it even more because I was now leaving the basement of my parents' house and going back to Chicago.

I was determined to never live here again. Being home had been nice, but it wasn't what it used to be, and I realized that was okay. At first it really bothered me, I thought this summer was going to be one big party or possibly a high school friend reunion, but I was wrong. This summer was nothing how I imagined it to be at all, but that's usually how all my summers have turned out to be. This summer consisted of working or being stuck in my mind replaying old memories or trying to conjure up my ideal future. Honestly, this had worked out for me. In the beginning, I wasn't in the best spot to be around others. I had to get myself together. Nothing would've been worse than faking being okay and having forced conversations while I wasn't fine. I was no longer a kid, and it dawned on me that those carefree summers were just a memory.

I was now an adult, well trying to be one. There was no more doing what I wanted to do all the time with countless hours of free time. I couldn't imagine myself having another summer like that until I'd worked hard enough to be rich and relax. I looked forward to that part of my life, but I knew I had some ways to go and hoped I figured it out soon.

I wanted to make sure I took the cutest clothes with me and not pack every single article of clothing

I owned and that included all those spirit week shirts from middle school that I wore for pajamas, a childish mistake I made last year. I cringed just thinking about walking around the building wearing them.

"Knowing you, I know you have some sort of plan for the upcoming school year."

"I do, hence the closet clean out," I said holding up a three-quarter sleeve black wrap dress that was totally made for me to parade around Chicago in.

Pushing back shirts and dresses I had hung along the pipes along the ceiling made me miss my walk-in in our previous home. I had my shoes aligned on the shelves, dresses, and tops hung on one side while my pants were displayed on the other. I often would lie there for hours when I was stressed or spent the majority of my Sunday evenings putting together my outfits for the upcoming week in high school. That was a luxury I was deadset on replacing when I got a place of my own.

"So what's on the agenda?"

"For starters, I'm keeping my options open in every category: friends, boys, job opportunities, literally everything. I felt like I was too closed-off last year, it was mostly nerves but still. I want everything to flow to me."

"Ooooh, ok I like. But what about Victor?"

Hmmmm, what about the young man? I had barely heard from him the whole summer and we left things so open they might as well have been closed.

"I have no clear direction on where to go with that, so I've decided to set my eyes on other destinations."

"Meaning?"

"Meaning, I'm pretty sure there are other guys that I could date besides Victor." I had no clear prospects as I spent most of my focus on him without giving anyone a real chance.

"But don't you love Victor? Also, can I have this red top?"

"Love is a strong word, and even though I have very deep feelings for him and share a connection. I'm not sure if love is the right word to describe what went on there. Yes, to the top."

"Do what you want, but I'm rooting for Victor."

"You make it sound like I'm on *The Bachelorette*, but of course you're rooting for Victor. You're a hopeless romantic."

I had a better vision of what I wanted. Although I approached most of my ventures with apprehension, I was a bit more confident than I had been before and a great way to express that was through my outfit choices. I decided on taking more dressy items rather than casual ones because I wanted to push myself to dress up more. By doing this I knew I wouldn't have a choice, I wanted to put a solid effort into every aspect of the school year.

I was calmer about the packing process this time around; I didn't have some master-packing list of what

I thought was important. It turned out that I didn't use more than half the things I brought last year. I wasn't messaging my roommates about who was bringing what, because we had that all figured out. I didn't have any apprehension about leaving. I was ready to go with no desire to stay. Last summer I remembered not wanting to leave my friends for fear that I wouldn't meet anyone else whom I loved hanging out with as much and who understood me. But I was wrong, I just didn't want to leave my bedroom and share a room with someone who could be strange, a psycho killer, or someone who watched *LMN* on a loop; those were fears freshmen had, and I was no longer one.

Last year, I was wrong about the psycho killer part, but one of my old roommates was strange. We never talked unless we discussed the bathroom schedule, whose turn it was to clean, or if I invited her to do things and she turned me down. I asked her to come with me to the lounge since they were serving milkshakes, and she said no because she didn't like milkshakes. I felt like she was lying, because I had never met someone in my entire life who didn't like milkshakes. That was my last attempt to try to hang out with her. She clearly had her mind made up not to become friends with me, so I never invited her to anything else again. If Savannah and my other roommate didn't live with us, I don't know how I would've survived.

I no longer felt obligated to anything here but my family. I loved Michigan and it would always be the place I called home. When I first left for Chicago, I felt stripped of a part of myself. In the beginning of the school year, I found myself missing going to the Franklin Hills Cider Mill at the start of the fall, going to see the Tigers play at Comerica Park stadium, and going to downtown Birmingham with my friends on the weekend. Those were traditions that I could no longer partake in, and they were a part of who I was for so long I didn't feel exactly like myself without them.

Then, anytime I came home for breaks I felt like I was being stripped of Chicago. I missed going to the Garfield Park Conservatory, spending hours at the Museum of Contemporary Art on Saturday afternoons, and eating Giordano's deep dish pizza.

These were now the things I was used to. These were *my* personal traditions, free from family and friend influence. I did these things alone while I didn't have any friends at all. During that time of solitude, I found out more of what I liked doing, and my experiences weren't being polluted by the opinions of others. I got to try new things without being hindered by other people's input. So many times in my life I didn't do something new or go somewhere new because of what someone I knew had to say. At first, I was freaked out by how much time I spent by myself, but without it I don't think I would've gotten to know myself better. Now I knew how important it was, because now I didn't mind spending time alone. I loved myself, I loved going to new places and doing new things and making myself think and see how I really felt about all that I was taking in.

Michigan was where I was from and where I grew up, it molded a lot of the way I was. But in Chicago, I felt my most independent. I felt like I was creating myself and in the process of becoming who I was meant to be. That is something I have wanted so badly, I was in love with the idea of being independent, strong, and self-aware. I wasn't completely there yet, but I was closer than I was before. It became a second home. For these reasons, both places would always have a special place in my heart no matter where my life took me.

starting

I exhaled with my hands on my hips looking out the window at my magnificent view, I was back where it all started. It was a new year, but I was in the same building, the feeling of nostalgia was overwhelmingly present. My family helped me unpack my dad's truck and bring everything to the eighteenth floor.

"Well Krista, one year older, and one floor higher," dad said happy to be done unpacking.

"Yeah, that's funny how that ended up working out."

"This view is amazing by the way. I can't wait to go here," Kathryn said as she was taking pictures on her phone.

"Great, maybe we could move from the townhouse into a one-bedroom apartment, so we can afford it," my dad said jokingly.

I didn't really feel like it was a joke, but everyone chose to ignore his comment.

"I'm just kidding guys, I'm really happy to see you here. I know you're going to do great things."

That's the thing about my dad, he came off as really stern, but he could be sweet. It was nice to hear him express that he was proud of me, and not make it all about money.

"Are you nervous?" my mom asked.

"Not really, I am a little, but it's a good nervous."

As we made our way back downstairs and outside, I noticed the Windy City wasn't that windy today, and it still felt like summer. I was going to enjoy it and take advantage of it; you never knew when the sun would disappear for a week at a time here.

I gave my little sister, mom, and dad a hug. A piece of me wished my older sister could've been here. She still hadn't contacted me. I was a bit worried but convinced myself she was fine because she was Valentina.

"Try not to miss us too much," my dad said yelling out the driver seat window.

"Don't forget to call us tonight, we want to know that you're all settled," my mom preached.

"Ok! I will!" I yelled back and waved goodbye. I was embarrassed we were doing this directly in front of the dorm while other students were wheeling cardboard boxes in and out of the building during move-in day.

"I love you, Krista!" Kathryn screamed at me and the rest of the city.

"I love you too!" I replied blushing.

The truck turned the corner and I watched it until it was out of sight.

There were no tears this time, just smiles. I'm pretty sure we were all smiling for different reasons though. I was smiling because I was back at school. My family was smiling because they wanted the best for me, and they felt like this place was going to get me there. This was my new normal, they were now used to me being gone and I was now used to being away. Last year this looked very different. When I watched them drive away it felt like I was being ripped apart. I was so excited about leaving that I didn't mentally or emotionally prepare for what being away from people I loved most was truly like. A year changed a lot of things; last year I was scared of all the change around me and this was the biggest risk I had ever taken. I was going to school in another state and didn't know one person who went here, but I knew this risk was going to be the only way I could grow. The process of growth was uncomfortable but the product was always worth it.

I walked back into the building and the same two security guards who worked the front desk last year smiled at me.

"Are you ready for this year?" the security guard named Glenda asked me. Her curly ponytail bounced as she shuffled behind the desk gathering a bulk of key cards for students who hadn't picked them up yet.

"Yeah," I said calmly, but on the inside, I was screaming it.

I approached the desk to get back my I.D. they collected as collateral, confirming you were the student moving into the correct apartment.

"Glad to see you again, have you run into your main man yet?"

The question hit me like a bullet as I purposefully pushed any thoughts about Victor out of my mind before they would completely take over and I would obsess again.

"Not yet, but I'm sure I'll see him around soon."

"Alright Krista, here you go. Welcome back!" she expressed happily as she handed over my identification card.

"Thank you." I smiled and turned and entered the hall where the elevators were located.

Walking to the elevator I thought about how I had worked my butt off to be there, depositing my $2,129.82 into my school account meant more to me than I could express. I worked day in and out at a place over the whole summer just to get back here.

As I got on and pressed eighteen, I thought about Victor and wondered if he was here yet, if he chose to stay in the same building, and when we would inevitably see each other. I chose to blame Glenda for that; I pushed the thought out as quickly as it came in.

I wasn't going to let my hard work and personal growth over the summer go to waste, not for Victor or anyone else. I felt like that was something I would've done last year, and this was a new year, and an improved version of Krista Clark. But in reality, I knew keeping my mind off Victor was going to be harder than anything else Sophomore year.

about the author

CHRISTIAN SANDRA-ELISE COOK is from the suburbs of Detroit. At age sixteen, she graduated high school and then attended Columbia College Chicago. Here, she obtained a BA in Public Relations and discovered her depth as a woman and a writer by taking various creative writing courses and using the city of Chicago as her campus. After being accepted into a writing program in Paris she rediscovered her passion for her first true love; writing. Paris was also Christian's first time traveling outside of the United States and it opened her eyes to new experiences, a slower pace, and it made her question life as she understood it. Always curious, Christian discusses life, faith, and all the unexpected occurrences in between.

CPSIA information can be obtained
at www.ICGtesting.com
Printed in the USA
JSHW061814160822
29342JS00003B/164